Praise for
WELCOME TO HARD TIMES

"A forceful, credible story of cowardice and evil."
The *Washington Post*

"We are caught up with these people as real humans.... This is a book you'll be hearing about."

Chicago Sun-Times

"A taut, bloodthirsty read."
Times Literary Supplement

Also by E. L. Doctorow:

BIG AS LIFE

THE BOOK OF DANIEL*

RAGTIME*

LOON LAKE*

LIVES OF THE POETS: Six Stories and a Novella

WORLD'S FAIR*

*Published by Fawcett Books

E. L. Doctorow

WELCOME TO HARD TIMES

FAWCETT CREST • NEW YORK

For Mandy

FIRST
LEDGER

ONE

THE MAN FROM BODIE DRANK DOWN A HALF BOT-
tle of the Silver Sun's best; that cleared the dust from
his throat and then when Florence, who was a red-
head, moved along the bar to him, he turned and
grinned down at her. I guess Florence had never seen a
man so big. Before she could say a word, he reached
out and stuck his hand in the collar of her dress and
ripped it down to her waist so that her breasts bounded
out bare under the yellow light. We all scraped our
chairs and stood up—none of us had looked at Florence that way before, for all she was. The saloon was
full because we watched the man coming for a long
time before he pulled in, but there was no sound now.

This town was in the Dakota Territory, and on three
sides—east, south, west—there is nothing but miles of
flats. That's how we could see him coming. Most times
the dust on the horizon moved east to west—wagon
trains nicking the edge of the flats with their wheels
and leaving a long dust turd lying on the rim of the
earth. If a man rode toward us he made a fan in the air
that got wider and wider. To the north were hills of
rock and that was where the lodes were which gave an
excuse for the town, although not a good one. Really
there was no excuse for it except that people naturally
come together.

3

So by the time he walked into the Silver Sun a bunch of us were waiting to see who he was. It was foolish because in this country a man's pride is not to pay attention, and after he did that to the girl he turned around to grin at us and we looked away or coughed or sat down. Flo meanwhile couldn't believe what happened, she stood with her eyes wide and her mouth open. He took his hand off the bar and suddenly grabbed her wrist and twisted her arm around so that she turned and doubled over with the pain. Then, as if she was a pet bear, he walked her in front of him over to the stairs and up to a room on the second floor. After the door slammed we stood looking up and finally we heard Florence screaming and we wondered what kind of man it was who could make her scream.

Jimmy Fee was the only child in town and when Flo was stumbling over her dress up the stairs, he ducked under the swinging doors and ran down the porch past the man's horse and across the street. Fee, his father, was a carpenter, he had built up both sides of the street almost without help. Fee was on a ladder fixing the eaves over the town stable.

"Pa," Jimmy called up to him, "the man's got your Flo!"

Jack Millay, the limping man with one arm, told me later he followed the boy across the street to fill Fee in on the details—little Jimmy might not have made it clear that the customer was a Bad Man from Bodie. Fee came down the ladder, went around in back of his place down the street, and came out with a stout board. He was a short man, bald, thick in the neck and in the shoulders, and he was one of the few men I ever met who knew what life was about. I was standing by the window of the Silver Sun and when I saw Fee coming I got out of those doors fast. So did everyone there, even though the screaming had not stopped. By the time Fee walked in with his plank at the ready, the place was empty.

We all stood scattered in the street waiting for something to happen. Avery, the fat barkeep, had brought a bottle with him and he tilted his head back and drank, standing out in the dirt with his white apron on and one hand on his hip. I had never seen Avery in sunlight before. The sun was on the western flats to about four o'clock. There was no sound now from the saloon. The only horse tied up in front was the stranger's: a big ugly roan that didn't look like he expected water or a rub. Behind him in the dirt was a pile of new manure.

We waited and then there was a noise from inside—a clatter—and that was all. After a while Fee came out of the Silver Sun with his cudgel and stood on the porch. He walked forward and missed the steps. The Bad Man's horse skittered aside and Fee tumbled down and landed on his knees in the manure. He got up with dung clinging to his britches and lurched on toward Ezra Maple, the Express Man, who said: "He can't see." Ezra stepped aside as Fee staggered by him. The back of Fee's bald head was bashed and webbed with blood and he was holding his ears. Little Jimmy stood next to me watching his father go up the street. He ran after a few yards, then stopped, then ran after again. When he caught up to Fee he took his belt and together they walked into Fee's door.

Nobody went back into the saloon, we were all reminded of business we had to do. When I got to my office door I glanced back and the only one still standing in the street was Avery, in his apron. I knew he'd be the first over to see me and he was.

"Blue, that gentleman's in my place, you got to get him out of there."

"I saw him pay you money Avery."

"I got stock behind that bar, I got window glass in my windows, I got my grain and still in back. There's no telling what he'll do."

"Maybe he'll leave soon enough."

"He cracked Fee's skull!"

"A fight's a fight, there's nothing I can do."

"Goddamnit!"

"Well now Avery I'm forty-nine years old."

"Goddamnit!"

I took my gun out of my drawer and shoved it over the desk toward fat Avery but he didn't take it. Instead he sat down on my cot and we waited together. About dusk Jimmy Fee came in and told me his father was bleeding at the mouth. I went out and found John Bear, the deaf-and-dumb Pawnee who served for our doctor, and we went over to Fee's place but Fee was already dead. The Indian shrugged and walked out and I was left to comfort the boy all night.

Once, around midnight, when it got too cold for me, I walked back to my office to get a blanket. And on the way I sneaked across the street—running where there was moonlight—to peek into the window of the Silver Sun. The lights were still burning. Behind the bar, Florence, with her red hair unpinned to her shoulders, was crying and pouring herself a stiff one. I tapped on the window, but she knew Fee was dead and she wouldn't come out. I ran around back. The upstairs was dark and I could hear the Man from Bodie snoring.

WHEN I CAME WEST WITH THE WAGON, I WAS A young man with expectations of something, I don't know what, I tar-painted my name on a big rock by the Missouri trailside. But in time my expectations wore away with the weather, like my name had from that rock, and I learned it was enough to stay alive. Bad Men from Bodie weren't ordinary scoundrels, they came with the land, and you could no more cope with them than you could with dust or hailstones.

I found twelve dollars in Fee's bureau when the sun came up and I gave them to Hausenfield, the German. Hausenfield owned a bathtub, he had brought it in his wagon all the way from St. Louis. At the beginning of each month Hausenfield would fill that tub with water from his well and sit right down in back of his house and wash. He also owned the stable.

After I gave him the money he went into his stable and pushed out his wagon by the tongue and hitched up his mule and his grey. The wagon was an old stage with the windows boarded and the seats torn out. It was black, the one painted thing in town. He drove it over to Fee's door.

"Put him in dere please."

Jack Millay, who was standing by with his one arm, helped me take Fee out and put him in the wagon.

"Don't you have a casket Hausenfield?"

"He never build me vun. He said he would build ten for me, but he never build even vun."

I closed the door on Fee and the wagon creaked down the street and into the flats. It was cold and early but nearly everyone was out watching it go. A pickaxe clanked on top of the stage, one of the wheels squeaked each time around, and the clanking and squeaking was Fee's funeral music. Hausenfield's grey pulled harder than his mule and so the wagon turned eastward slowly in an arc. About a mile out in the flats it stopped. Behind the wagon, from the southeast, rain clouds were coming up under the sky. I didn't know where Florence was but Jimmy Fee began to walk out after, now, with his hands in his pockets.

"Look there Blue!"

Across the street, in front of the saloon, the Bad Man's roan stood shivering where he'd been tied since yesterday.

"Cold got that man's horse," Jack Millay said, "he never did see to it." Even as Jack spoke the horse went down on its knees. That was all we needed—I wanted the man to go away with no difficulty, no trouble to himself. I walked into my office to think, and a few minutes later some fool who couldn't bear to see animals suffer but who didn't care if people did, stood a good safe way from the Silver Sun, probably behind some porch, and shot his carbine at the roan.

When I ran out the roan was twitching on his side and the street was empty.

"Who in hell did that!" I shouted.

Then, in a minute the Bad Man from Bodie came out of the saloon buckling his gun belt. I didn't move a muscle. He looked down at his horse and scratched his head and that was when I stepped slowly back inside my door and closed it. On the back wall of my office, behind my cot, there was another door and I went out that way.

I found Avery standing near my outhouse talking to his other girl, Molly Riordan. Along with the rest of us

Molly scooted out of the Silver Sun when the man had taken Flo. She sheltered for the night with Major Munn, the old veteran who liked to call her his daughter; and now Avery had her back and they were arguing.

"You're a son of a bitch, Avery," she said to him. Molly was never to my taste, pale and pocked, with a thin mouth and a sharp chin, but I liked the way she stood up to Avery.

"Blue, this son of a bitch wants me to go across there and get ripped open by that big bastard."

"Not so loud Molly, for God's sake!" Avery said.

"How do you like this fat-assed son of a bitch? He's some man, isn't he Blue?"

"Molly I got stock behind that bar; I got all my money under the counter. I'm telling you everything I got is in there." To make his point Avery slapped Molly hard across the face and when she put her hand to her cheek and began weeping, he pulled a stiletto from under his apron and held it out until she took it.

"You go on over there and when he holds you around, bring the knife out of your sleeve and put it in his neck. I can't have that gentleman in my place, I want him out of there."

Just then a hoot and a holler came from the street. I looked down the alley in time to see the Bad Man prancing by sideways on a big bay. He was on Hausenfield's good horse.

"He's not in your place now, Avery," I said.

T HE BAD MAN WAS CELEBRATING THE NEW DAY riding bareback back and forth from one end of the street to the other. Jack Millay met me in the alley: "Hausenfield left his barn door open."

"Too bad for Hausenfield."

"That man just walked over and took the bay for his own."

We watched from the shade: he kicked the horse this way and that, yelling and whooping through the street. When the horse got accustomed, he spurred him up the steps of the Silver Sun and then rode along the porch, ducking low for the beams. The horse kicked over the sack of dried beans in front of Ezra Maple's store and then jumped back into the street, and the Bad Man laughed and yelped some more. I was hoping he'd stop soon, saddle up, and then go riding toward the lodes. The clouds were moving from the south and if it rained he couldn't poke a horse up on wet rocks, even if he had a horse. But when he stopped it was at the north end of the street where John Bear had his shack.

John Bear did his cooking on the outside over a stone fire. Next to his shack he had a small plot he had worked on so that it gave up a few tubers and onions. John was squatting by his fire, cooking up some meal, when the man walked into his patch, stepping all over the plants. If John was deaf and dumb what he saw was enough. The man pulled up half a dozen plants before he found an onion that suited him. He wrung it free of its green and wiped it and peeled it and then bit in.

"Breakfast," I said to Jack Millay.

The man ignored John Bear as if he wasn't there. He stepped over to the Indian's fire and lifted up the skillet and walked away with it to sit down with his back against the shack. The Indian didn't move but just looked into his fire.

Avery and Molly Riordan were standing behind me, watching.

"Here's your chance to get back to your place, Avery."

"I don't know, Blue."

"Why don't you just walk across and go on in?"

"He'll see me."

Jack said: "Shit, Avery."

"Don't run and you'll be alright. Molly you get inside somewhere. I think you better not be seen."

Avery walked across stiff-legged, trying not to run, and I saw the Bad Man glance up for a moment from his eating. When Avery got inside the Silver Sun he closed the full doors in back of the swinging ones and pulled shades down over the windows.

"Now what's that man gonna do when he finds Avery's bolted the door?" Jack said.

I took a deep breath and walked out into the sun myself. I headed across the street, stepping around the man's dead roan, and when I got to the porch I coughed and went into Ezra Maple's store.

Ezra was standing by his window looking at the spilled sack of beans.

"He still sitting there?"

"Yep."

"I'll take some plug, Ezra."

"Help y'self."

I went behind the counter: "Ezra I want to ask you when the stage is due."

"A week. Maybe two."

"Well now what day is this? We get a fair crowd from the mines Saturday night."

"That's true. . . ."

"Well what day is this?"

"Thursday."

11

I walked over to the window and looked with Ezra at the spillings on his porch: the beans could have been flocks of birds flying high, southerly.

"Not much country, Blue."

"I took some cartridges with the plug."

In a while we saw Hausenfield driving his hearse hard into town, pulling on the grey's traces and whipping his mule. He stopped in front of the store and came in, tripping and cursing.

"Are you here, Blue? You have to do something!"

"Tell me what, Hausenfield."

"Dat is my horse he has."

"I saw."

"Are you not the mayor!"

"Only to those who voted for me." Ezra smiled when I said that: I had not been elected mayor, I had taken it upon myself to keep records in case the town ever got large enough to be listed, or in case statehood ever came about. I kept the book and they called me mayor.

Hausenfield looked at Ezra and smiled back: "Dat is alright," he said, "I have my veapon."

He stalked out and got his gun from his wagon. To this day I don't know whether Hausenfield meant to shoot the Bad Man or not. Probably, he didn't know himself. His horse was standing in John Bear's patch eating off the tops of the plants. Hausenfield marched down there and grabbed a fistful of mane and began leading the horse back to his stable. When he'd gone a few yards, he turned almost as an afterthought and shot twice at the Bad Man who sat watching him— once into the dirt in front of the man, once into the wood above him. The horse reared then and pulled away. Hausenfield fell down in the dust and I thought he would fire again from the ground; but I saw him crawling and trying to get up at the same time, waving his pistol at the horse and shouting in German. This put his back to the stranger who was up and running low, squeezing off rounds into his legs.

Faster than a cat the man was on top of Hausenfield, straddling him with his gun holstered now and swinging at his face with the flat of the skillet.

"He never let go of that pan," Ezra whispered.

Hausenfield had begun to scream when the bullets hit him but the man swung at his face until he could only moan. After a while the man threw the skillet away and looked up: the bay horse had cantered over to his stablemates in front of the black wagon and that must have given the man his idea. Laughing, he dragged Hausenfield by the collar over to the wagon and threw him in. This happened right in front of Ezra's window so we had to step back in the shadows. The man closed the door, found Hausenfield's pickaxe, still caked with the dirt of Fee's grave, and used it to bolt the door tight. Inside the hearse, Hausenfield was screaming again, pounding on the floorboard. The man jumped up on the driver's box, brought the grey and the mule around, and began to rein-whip them down the street. Hooting loud, he rode them close to the porch on the other side, and at the last porch beam at the end of the street, he hooked his arm around and stood easily on the rail while the wagon kept on going into the flats. To make sure that the team kept its pace he fired a few shots after it and even the mule ran with his ears back.

Walking to the bay in front of Ezra's store, the man was laughing to himself and smacking his hands together. Every few steps he would turn around to look at the wagon rumbling away south and each time he looked he laughed harder. He took the bay over to the

Silver Sun and saddled it with the gear from his dead roan. Then he tied his new horse to the rail, mopped his forehead with a red handkerchief and stepped up to the saloon doors, which he found locked. He kicked them open and from where I was I heard Avery's voice say heartily: "Come in, come in!"

AFTER THE MAN HAD BEEN A WHILE IN THE Silver Sun, everyone began to come out of doors, standing in ones and twos on the porch or in the street, watching that wagon going away smaller and smaller ahead of its dust cone. Jack Millay saw me and limped over swinging his one arm: "Did you ever see such work, Blue?" Jack's face was pinked with excitement, he took his joys how he could. In the alleys some of the people were bringing their buckboards to their side doors and at the rock end of the street John Bear had his travois lying in front of his shack.

I watched the Indian now. When Hausenfield had taken his pot shots Bear had jumped for cover fast enough although his back was turned to the noise. If he was deaf he had another sense to make up for it, if he was dumb he wasn't too dumb. He came out of his shack and lashed his things to the travois. Then he picked up the poles and pulled. When he reached his skillet lying in the middle of the street he walked right over it and he went right down the street and past the last house. Later I saw him standing half a mile in the flats. He laid his travois down and stood still facing the town.

Behind him and east, tiny Jimmy Fee who had never come back in was sitting by his father's grave.

Clouds were over half the sky now, the sun was covered and a little breeze was blowing.

I went to my office and found Molly Riordan looking in my desk.

"Haven't you any whiskey, Blue?"

"Whiskey's across the street," I said and just then we heard Avery yelling with a laugh in his voice: "Molly! Moll-y-y!"

Molly ducked behind the desk, and through a hole in my oilpaper window I saw Avery holding his swinging doors open, bellowing with good nature: "Molly where are you, gentleman here wants to see you!" Even across the street I could hear the bottle crashing somewhere behind him. He laughed as if he was enjoying it, called Molly again and went back in.

"Christ!" said Molly. "Isn't anybody going to do anything?"

"Why don't you go on over?"

"What?" She stood up then, watching me fill the cylinders of my gun.

I said: "That knife Avery gave you. Do as he said, hold it tight against your wrist and if your moment comes slip it out and use it. But I don't think you'll have to."

"Oh sure, sure! Christ that Bad Man's the only man in town! I can't believe it, you're no better than that son of a bitch Avery, using a lady, for Godsake, marching brave behind a lady's skirts. You're some comfort Mayor, go to hell!"

I tucked the gun in my belt and opened the door. People were waiting in the street.

"Oh God," Molly said, "so this is what it's come to, how did I ever end up in this forsaken town, oh Christ this is the end. I'll tell you something you didn't know, Blue, I left New York ten years ago because I couldn't bear bein' a maid, I was too proud to say 'Yes Mum.' Doesn't that tickle you?"

"We do what we can, Molly."

Her face was twisted up and tears were streaming down her cheeks as she walked by me saying: "I hope he gets you Mayor, I swear I do, you and the rest of the crawling bastards in this miserable town."

I followed behind her as we walked across—everyone stepping out of our way—and went up on the steps to the Silver Sun. She turned to look at me once more.

"You're alright, Molly," I said.

But when she walked up to the doors the stiletto slipped out of her sleeve and clattered on the porch. I kicked it aside before the Bad Man might see it and I pushed Molly through the doors and stepped in behind. Then I saw what made her drop the knife, Florence bent over the upstairs railing bare, with her arms dangling and her red hair falling down between them.

Now Avery must have seen the woman dead that way when he came back to close his doors and pull his shades down. But he wasn't too concerned when we came in, he greeted us laughing and jovial.

"Here's Molly, hello Blue! Come on, come in, drinks on the gentleman!"

Behind the bar the Bad Man from Bodie was grinning and setting up two more glasses. Avery went to the doors and opened them, calling into the street: "Everybody! Drinks for the whole town on the gentleman here!" The Bad Man laughed but outside everyone began to run, I could see under the doors the feet running in the dirt. The only one Avery got was Jack Millay, who had followed us onto the porch and was peeking over the doors when Avery shouted out his invitation. Avery pulled Jack in and I know that in a few minutes the town was empty but for those of us in the saloon.

It was a celebration. Avery, Jack Millay and I stood at the bar while the man poured for us. Molly sat at one of the tables staring up at Flo with her knuckles in her mouth. The man came around the bar and served her a drink from a tray, making a mock bow like a fancy Eastern waiter. She sat looking away from him and didn't even stir when he took the bottom of her skirt between two fingers and threw it back over her knees. Avery laughed at that and Jack laughed too and the man backed away from Molly, looking at her and chuckling. He went behind the bar again and lifted his glass to her.

The Bad Man drank Avery's liquor like water and every time he poured for himself, he poured for us too. The other two kept up with him but I emptied my glass by throwing the stuff over my shoulder. The man finally saw me do that and then he broke the neck off a fresh bottle and filled my glass slowly and then raised his and looked me in the eyes. He was a younger man than I expected but his skin was shot red under the stubble, there was a blaze on one cheek and he had the eyes of a crazy horse. Right then my hand began to move and I meant for it to go for my gun. But it went instead for the glass on the bar; I felt at that moment that I wanted to please him, I was almost glad to drink.

After that the man began to break open a bottle for each round. One time, as Avery had his drink up to his mouth, the man stuck his arm out and whacked Avery's glass with the heel of his hand. Avery stumbled back, spitting out teeth and blood and trying to laugh at the same time. A bit later, the man fixed his attention on Jack Millay's stump and with an eyewide amazement he swung at it with a full bottle of whiskey. Jack went grey and sunk to the floor right where he was standing.

I suppose it would have been my turn next but then his eye caught Molly again, sitting just as he'd left her.

He gave the rebel yell and jumped over the bar.

"Blue!" Molly screamed. She was trying to put tables and chairs between them and the Bad Man was laughing and tossing the furniture aside; Jack Millay was out on the footrail and Avery was slumped at the bottom of the stairs, crying and wiping at the blood on his apron. I drew my gun at that moment but it was too late. The man caught Molly by the wrist and almost at the same time I sent my shot, wild, across the room, he was crouched in front of her and shooting back. Molly was struggling and pulling or I'm sure he would have killed me; as it was his shots drove me through the doors, I fell back onto the porch and rolled off into the dirt. I heard him coming to the doors, laughing, and I picked up my hat and began running, stumbling, down the street, staying close to the porch and keeping low. He was at the doors now, sending shots into the dirt at my heels, into the porch alongside me, and what I thought then was that I wanted those records in my desk, I wanted to go across to my room and get those ledgers to safekeeping. But it was almost as if he knew, his bullets tore up the ground on my right and kept me going straight, I was limping from the pain of my fall, tripping in the dirt, my heart like a hand clenching my insides, and I didn't stop until I was out in the flats with everyone else.

So WE ALL STOOD SCATTERED ON THE FLATS LOOKing back at the town—the boy Jimmy Fee, John Bear, Ezra, and the rest—some with gear, some by a horse or a buckboard, some with bundles and some, like me, with nothing. Overhead the sky was heavy with clouds, a wind was blowing, and although it couldn't have been much past noon, the day was black. We watched for a long time. Every once in a while we could hear a scream or something crashing, small sounds now in the flats. And then, after a long silence, flames began to lick out of the saloon. Hausenfield's horse in front whinnied and pulled back on his ties and then the Bad Man came carrying a chair on fire. He whooped and threw the chair across and it landed on the porch in front of my office. Then he saw something and ran across the street. What he saw was Fee's ladder still leaning where it was left against the stable. He picked up that ladder and went around poking out windows with it and when the wind had caught the flames and both sides of the street were framed in fire, he used the ladder to knock down the porch beams, jumping aside and hollering when the hot wood fell into the street.

But then the bay was going mad so he untied him and got on his back and held him to a walk toward the rocks. We couldn't see the man for a long while after that, but finally Ezra Maple pointed to the hills: He was well up on the trail toward the lodes, lighted for a moment by the fire down below him, picking his way through the stone and not even looking back. He disappeared again and that was all we saw of the Bad Man from Bodie, though we waited to make sure. The rain finally began to come down hard and we stood watching it fall into the fire and watching the fire lick up at the rain.

TWO

THE SILVER SUN MADE THE BRIGHTEST FLAME AND the cleanest smoke. Once or twice part of the roof blew into the air above the fire—and that would be Avery's kegs of alcohol. By and by the rain began to let up. The wind came back and whiffs of the smoke blew out on the flats. Off to the left of me Major Munn, the veteran who liked to call Molly Riordan daughter, was standing up on his buckboard with his arm raised. He was a bent old man with long white mustaches, and he was yelling into the smoke and roar which came out to us on the wind: "If I'd had you before me at Richmond, I'd have put the ball in yer eye, God help you, I killed twenty like you when I was younger," his voice piped over the flats. "Let the sun drop you in the badlands and let you not die before the shit of prairie dogs is in yer mouth and the buzzard's claw is on yer belly. May yer pizzle fry in Hell and your eggs wither to peas, may the marrow boil in yer bones and yer eyes melt in their holes for what you done here, God damn you, God damn you..." He was shaking his fist toward the town but for a moment I had the feeling it was me he was cursing.

Then the fire's roar smothered his words, and a gust of smoke hid him from my sight. When it cleared again I saw that Major was not up behind his horse, but down on the ground under him. I ran over: he had toppled with a stroke, his fist was still rigid, there was froth on his lips and a rattle in his throat. I put my hand on him and his eyes opened and he stared at me and died.

Someone leaning over my back said: "Well I have seen the elephant." Others came to look at the Major and it was enough to break the spell of the fire. People began tying down their gear, pulling cinches tight. In a few minutes half the town was strung out across the flats, only the women in the wagons looking back.

THE RAIN DIDN'T HURT WHAT FIRE THERE WAS BUT it cut the wind down and that saved two structures: in the back of what had been Hausenfield's place the gawky windmill over his well was still standing; and at the far end of the town, near the rocks, the Indian's shanty was untouched. By the time the sun came out again everything else was gone, only some quarter posts still stood, charred and half eaten, and also one or two half-burned house sides where Fee had used green lumber.

When I walked back a few little fires were still working along the ground and smoke from the ruins was rising straight up into the sky. The street was covered with ashes and everywhere you looked there were mice running in circles, dozens of squeaking little miseries twisting around in the dirt, flopping from their bellies to their backs. A jackrabbit was jumping into the air, trying to get off a jumble of glowing timbers, but he couldn't jump clear. I almost expected one-armed Jack to come tugging at my sleeve to tell me what a fine sight that was.

Stepping high over the rubble I found my desk upended and smoking. The drawers were burnt out and I found just the covers left of my ledgers. My mattress was gone too, it was a corn-husk mattress, the best I ever slept on. The only other thing of mine I could identify was a patch of brown blanket. The desk and the blanket and the ledgers I had bought from a lawyer who had passed through a year before, dumping everything he owned so as to march on unencumbered up to the mining camp in the lodes.

I kicked around in the debris and finally saw something else: it was my habit to keep my fortune of two pouches of gold dust under the floor of my office, but the pouches were gone and my dust stood in two solid cakes. Those nuggets sat there like somebody's eggs. There were other people poking around in the rubble up and down the street and I wondered what any of them would say if they found a pair of balls lying independent like that. I tried to pick up the gold but it crumbled and spilled and I only got a few pinches into my pockets. I didn't try to reclaim the rest, after just a few minutes in this smoke and heat my face was grimy, my eyes were watering and my clothes were about dry although the rain had left me drenched. There was a terrible stench over everything that made me remember the people lying under the Silver Sun.

All that was left of the saloon were the three steps leading up to the porch, and there was a small fire under them. Just beyond, up where his store had been, Ezra Maple was taking inventory, pushing boards aside, kicking his ruined goods. He was the one who saw Molly lying on the ground in back of the saloon rubble.

"Blue! Look here!"

She was lying face down, the whole back of her dress was burned away. I kneeled down by her side and after looking hard I was sure she was breathing.

"She's alive," I said to Ezra.

"Well what do you mean to do?"

"We can't leave her here this way."

I straightened up and saw John Bear pulling his travois back down the street toward his shack. I yelled at him but he didn't turn around so I had to run and get him. The three of us picked Molly up by the hands and feet and carried her over to the Indian's hut. The front of her dress hung down like a flag.

"Wait a minute," Ezra said, wanting to stop, "it's not decent."

"You can't cover her up," I said, "her whole back is burned." From her shoulder blades to her ankles, Molly was covered with blisters. We laid her down on the hard earth inside Bear's place and then the Indian went out and drew some water from Hausenfield's tank. When he came back he scraped a pile of earth from his floor and poured the water on it till it was a mush; then he took a tin from his pack and sprinkled whatever was in that tin—saleratus maybe—on the mud; then he spread the mixture along Molly's back and haunches and legs and covered it up with some kind of flat weed he had. John Bear was a true doctor, there was no hesitation in his moves. By the time he was finished Molly was moaning, a good sound although I didn't like to hear it. I stepped outside and a shadow passed over my eyes.

I don't know where the buzzards come from but

they're never late. Three or four were making slow circles above the town, another few over the flats. I had left the Major's body out there, lodged against a back wheel so his pony couldn't run. But one of the carrion birds glided down, spread his big wings and perched on the buckboard and I saw the pony shy. A second later I heard his whinny and then he was rearing; the wheel rolled over the Major, and the pony was trotting free toward the town, pulling the rig with him, leaving the old man's body exposed to the birds.

A few hundred yards to the east the little boy, Jimmy Fee, was running around his father's grave, waving his arms as if the shadows of the buzzards were cobwebs in his hair.

I ran to the end of the street and caught the horse, turned him around and rode him back out. The birds on Major Munn spraddled their wings and flapped into the air. They had already blooded his neck. I lifted the old man on the buckboard, sitting him down among his possessions. There was a blanket and I threw it over him. Then I rode the wagon to Jimmy Fee. A few more buzzards had come up over the flats and now they circled Fee's grave in a procession. Hausenfield had not dug very deep. The boy was huddled on top of the mound with his hands over his head, he was crying and screaming although he had hardly whimpered when Fee died.

"Come on up here, boy," I said still holding the reins. "Come on up beside me." But he only cried the more. I had to step down and carry him in my arms and hold him in my lap all the way back to town. He kept crying: "They're gonna get my Pa, the birds are gonna get my Pa...." And I knew that before anything else we had better hurry up and bury the dead. Someone in the street was shooting and cursing and a coyote was running fast back to the rocks.

EZRA FOUND ONE SHOVEL FROM HIS STORE THAT was only charred along the haft, and I found a rusty pick that was lying at the foot of Hausenfield's windmill. To give Jimmy Fee something to do I sent him looking for his own digging tool and he came on the skillet lying in the dirt where the Bad Man had flung it. Even if we had ten new shovels it would have done no good, only two of the men besides Ezra and me were willing to help dig. The rest of those who had come back to the town were packing their saddles or loading their rigs with what was left to them and riding out in ones and twos.

I chose to dig in the flats, making the holes in a line beginning with Fee's. There is no work harder than cutting a grave. Though the rain had softened the ground, it was a few hot hours of taking turns at the pick and shovel before we had the five holes dug. The bodies we had gathered were lying under blankets. When it came time to put them down and to rebury Fee I didn't want the boy there, I shooed him away. We stood waiting while he walked back, turning every few yards to look at us. He finally squatted down at the edge of the flats, not going as far as the town, I suppose, because the buzzards were all down in the street now eating from that dead roan.

We did what we had to and the two men besides Ezra and me got on one horse and rode off south. Everyone else had already left. I wiped my forehead with my sleeve, the sun was low in the west but I was warm. My foot ached and flies were buzzing around my head.

"Shall we say a word, Ezra?"

"Expect so."

"Well what should it be?"

He took his hat off and I took off mine and we stood looking down at the fresh earth: There is great human shame when people die before they are ready. It's as if their living didn't matter at all. I thought of Fee putting his trust in wood, and fat Avery worrying for his establishment, and crippled Jack with a one-armed interest in things; I thought of the old Major who always wore his dress blues on Sunday; and I thought of the way redheaded Flo, who had plump knees, could sometimes get interested. I had been in the town a year and I knew them all. Behind me the town was now a ruin, and who would remember in another year that it was ever there or that they had ever lived?

The Bad Man's grinning face came back to me and I felt my shy hand choosing the glass he offered. Twenty years before I had put my young wife into the ground after the cholera took her and the same rage rose in my throat for something that was too strong for me, something I could not cope with.

Kicking a clod with his toe Ezra said: "Well the Lord says blessed are the meek for they shall inherit the earth."

WE RODE BACK IN TO HAUSENFIELD'S WELL TO wash the grave dirt off. Jimmy Fee followed us and squatted with his back against the bottom of the windmill, but he wouldn't wash and he wouldn't look at us.

I saw from where I stood that it would not do to leave that dead roan lying in the middle of the street. He was covered with the birds and I knew if the birds flew off he would be covered with bluebottle flies. When I finished washing I said to Ezra: "Between your mule and the Major's pony I think they could just about pull that carcass out of here."

"Where to?"

"Down along the rocks about a mile."

"No sense to that," Ezra said, "unless you're fixin' to stay."

"I am." I had hoped he was too.

He looked at me: "Town's gone, Blue."

"Now I don't know," I said. "We got a cemetery. That's the beginnings of a town anyway."

Ezra poured half a bucket of water over his head. Then he wiped his face and neck with a rag, and then his arms and hands.

"Blue, I came West from Vermont. They have trees in that country."

"Is that right?"

"Water flows from the rocks, game will nibble at your back door, and if you're half a man you can make your life without too much trouble."

"That's what I once heard about this country."

"That's what I heard too. Back in Vermont."

Ezra was a long-faced man, taller than I was, with a stoop in his shoulders and eyes like a beagle hound. He put on a coat and turned to look at the black smoking street and the scrubby stretches beyond:

"Truth is, if the drought don't get you and the blizzards don't get you, that's when some devil with liquor in his soul and a gun in his claw will ride you down and clean you out."

27

He walked over to his mule, fixed his saddle and climbed on. With his hunched shoulders and his long coat and sad eyes Ezra was not much of a sight on muleback.

"There are other towns westerly," he said. "A man's a fool if he don't know when to move on."

And I said: "Ezra, all my life I have been moving along. I have trailed cattle from Texas to Kansas, I have whacked bulls for Russell and Waddell, I have placer mined for myself through the Black Hills, I have seen minstrel shows in Cheyenne and played poker in Deadwood and Leadville and Dodge, I have moved from one side of the West to the other, like a pebble rolling in the pan, and if you think this place here is not much country I can tell you none of it is."

He was looking down at Jimmy Fee: "Come with me if you like, sonny. I'll teach you to storekeep."

Jimmy sat there on his haunches, poking a twig in the dirt.

"So be it," Ezra said. He kicked his mule and rode off.

Well I couldn't waste time watching Ezra go, I had only an hour's light to do something about that stinking horse. I couldn't move him with just the little rig pony, it seemed the only thing to do was throw dirt on and make him a hill. So I did, piling ashes and dirt alongside his back and building up from there. Overhead the buzzards were turning, not too happy, and each time I threw a spadeful on the carrion, a horde of flies buzzed up around me.

I finished by sundown and my back was sore. I rubbed it some and that's when I realized the gun in my belt was gone. At first I thought I had dropped it but then I noticed little Jimmy was nowhere about. I walked over to the Indian's shack.

John Bear was on his knees making some more medicine pack, and Molly was crying on the buffalo rug. An oil lamp was in the corner but the boy was not there. I went outside and looked up to the rocks. Sure enough, there he was scrabbling along, waving the gun in his hand, he was going after the Bad Man from Bodie.

It was something to bring him back, I had to do it so he wouldn't shoot himself or me trying to get along that trail. I caught up with him and grabbed him from behind and carried him back down while he kicked and clawed. He was light but he fought hard, and he didn't begin to whimper until I threw him down in a corner of Bear's shack.

I sat down myself to draw a breath. But Bear built up a small pit fire and by its light, Molly—turning her head in pain—strangled a wail in her throat and locked my eyes in a terrible green gaze. A moment later she was crying again and the boy was crying too and the night breeze started to moan through the shanty boards like an awful chorus of ghosts, and with all that misery in such small space I thought for one second to get up and get out of there and ride away fast. But I could no more do that than Fee and Flo and the others could get up from their graves—the Bad Man had fixed us all in the spot and he had fixed me by leaving me alive. Before long I could hear the coyotes jumping down from the rocks and panting past the shack over to the dead horse. They snarled and scratched and when I looked out the door I could see their shadows throwing up dirt all over the hill. Smoke still rose, blue now in the moonlight, and embers were glowing on the ground like peepholes to Hell.

THREE

Now the saying is common that Sam Colt made men equal. But if it is true then our town wouldn't have burned up in the rain; instead that Bad Man would have been buried with due honors and a proper notice sent to the Territory Office. He would have had a hole in his chest, or his back, and the one who shot him would have Avery standing him a drink and maybe redheaded Flo and Molly smiling his way. Colt gave every man a gun, but you have to squeeze the trigger for yourself.

A few times during that long cold night I thought the Bad Man was coming back. The Major's pony, tethered outside, would whinny or snort, or some pebbles would roll down from the rocks, or Molly would cry out as if he was walking through the door. But really there was nothing he would come back for: in the morning I went out to stomp the numbness from my feet, and my eyes felt the shock of seeing air where the town had been. The chilly dawn rested right on the charred ground, the flats began at the horizon and came up to where I stood. I could not see a soul.

I was stiff and sore and bleary from no sleep and my first breath of the frosty morning sent a pain into my stomach. I went over to the ruins of Ezra Maple's store and started to poke around. Jimmy Fee woke up and came out of the shack and stood watching me while he made water in the middle of the street. He had his father's wide-set eyes, the Fee look on his face that took you in but didn't ask any questions, and his hair needed to be cut so bad that his head looked too large for his body. I had never seen such a skinny boy.

"Are you hungry?" I called, but he didn't answer.

Two fallen planks lay like hands with their fingers touching and under them I found some dried apples and peas in the ashes. The peas were well roasted.

"Jimmy, look around for a coffeepot, find us a pot, boy."

That was the way to talk to him, he went right to it. I had not picked a handful of peas out of the ashes before he was running up with a good pot. We drew some water and washed the soot off and I built a fire out of China matches from my pocket and we brewed up some pea coffee. With the apples it helped the hunger, but it tasted bad enough to make me remember all the good coffee I had drunk in my life and the beef and bacon and bread I had eaten.

I took some of the breakfast into the shack but Molly was asleep. She had cried almost until dawn. She lay with her arms out in front of her, thin and white, and her matted hair was caked at the tips with Bear's mud medicine. The Indian was sitting by her side, chewing on some dried corn. I put down the pot and the apples and went back outside to scavenge with the boy.

We recovered two charred tins of milk from Ezra's store, a tomato can, a box of .45 shells, the head of a hammer, a handful of horseshoe nails and a hunk of lye soap. From the remains of the Silver Sun we picked out a length of balustrade, three oil lamps—one with the glass unbroken—and lots of black bottles and chipped glasses. Elsewhere we found a charred saddle and a round stove, intact, and Jimmy even came up with an almanac that was only burnt around the edges. As we hunted the sun rose warm and took the chill out of my back, and by noon we had a pile of goods sitting in front of Bear's shanty.

But I didn't want to spend another night there.

I stepped inside to see if Molly was awake. Slits and speckles of light lay across the floor and one strip of light fell on her open eyes. She looked bad. Her face was so thin I could see how the bones and blue veins went under her skin. The food beside her was untouched. I didn't know what to say to her, I didn't know what she would say to me, but I said:

"Molly I'm going to build a dugout over by the well. Earth is the one thing we've got in supply and a good sod wall will do better against the weather than these boards will."

For a second I thought she was dead, she was so still. Then she was whispering something and I bent down to hear:

"A man gave me a little trinket once. On a chain. I left it with the Major to hold."

I lowered my own voice: "Molly, I must tell you the old man is dead."

"Ah," her eyes closed, "I knew. . . ."

"He died of a fit, he was cursing the Bad Man. Wait—"

The pony was in the flats grazing on what he could, I had sent Jimmy out on his back after our salvage; but the Major's rig was outside the door and under the seat I found a carved box of private things—pearl buttons, a tin of mustache wax, a collar, a Union medal and a small cross on a chain.

I brought the cross in to Molly. I held it out to her

and she reached up and gently took it from me with her long fingers and clutched it tight as she laid her head back down on her hands. Then she smiled. My heart jumped with that smile and I asked her would she eat something.

"Take care of me Blue?" she said softly.

"Yes Molly, if you allow."

Still smiling she said "Mayor"—whispering so that I bent down and put my ear almost to her lips—"if I had that knife now I wouldn't drop it. I would stick it in you and watch the yellow flow."

For a moment I didn't understand, I could not reconcile the words with the smile on her face. But I looked at her and saw what a sweet smile it was, full of hate, and I felt as if I had been swiped to the ground by the paw of a big cat.

John Bear was turning over his garden patch with a piece of rock and he came around to the door just as I stepped out. I pushed by him without a word. The shovel was where I had left it, over by the offal. The coyotes had scalloped out one side of the dirt mound and eaten clear down to the bone. I knew they would be back at night for the rest, but I had to throw new dirt on anyway. An awful sense of hopelessness came over me. In this ruin and desolation, the ache of all my years rose in my bones and I was ready to sit down where I was and give up the ghost. What was the use? The woman in John Bear's shack was no longer Molly, what had happened in Avery's saloon could never be undone. The only hope we have is that we can pay off on our failures, and Molly's grin had burned the hope right out of me.

My hands were sore gripping the shovel again, they had swelled and blistered from all the grave-digging yesterday, it was only their needling distress which made me hold on tight as I could and march with that shovel over to the windmill. For no other reason than the pain shooting up my arms did I stick the blade into the ground and begin laying out a dugout.

This windmill was the one thing of value that the Bad Man had left. Hausenfield had paid to have the well drilled and then he had made back his costs by charging everybody for the water. It was either the German's good well water or the tepid stored from a rain or a long climb to a trickle spring up in the rocks. Most people paid. Fee had met the charge by building Hausenfield's stable, Avery had used his girls. Some others took what they needed when Hausenfield wasn't looking. I cut an eight-foot square near the windmill and wet it down with pails of water. I dug blocks of sod and piled them on the line. By digging four feet down and piling the sod two feet high you were sure of a ceiling you could stand under if you didn't stretch. Jimmy Fee came riding in on the pony's back and he gave the animal a drink. He held the bridle and watched me dig.

"You makin' another grave?" he said.

Well I felt I was. But I said, "Hitch up that pony and find us some lumber you can't break. I'm making a place to live."

B Y MID-AFTERNOON THERE WAS A DEAD HOT SUN in the sky. I took my shirt off and put a cloth around my neck and as I worked I lifted my hat every few minutes to let the air in. There was no wind and the water in the tank went down and I had to climb the scaffold to turn those stubby mill blades. The digging and the climbing wore on me, I had worked all my life but the year I had lived in the town I had grown soft as I thought I had a right to do in my old age. I felt that year now. Luckily for me, Bear came out of his shack to take a nap in its shade side, and afterwards he walked over and without a word gave me a spell on the shovel. I guess he didn't want me in his place any more than I wanted to be there. The digging was done by sundown.

We found a fairly good shake in the rubble and dragged it over for a ridgepole. When it was in place I laid the odd bits of lumber Jimmy had collected across from the shake to the sod walls. Then I laid other wood over the cracks. Then we went up to the rocks and brought back armfuls of scrub and covered the boards and threw some dirt on and there was a dugout, roof and all. Of course it lacked a door for the hole on one side, but that was a refinement which could wait. What I wanted now was to set up the stove inside and eat some of the apples and maybe open one tin of the milk.

I said to Jimmy: "Get in there and jump a little, tamp that floor down." I had learned early in the morning that he was alright as long as you ordered him about. All day I had been telling him what to do and he had done it. This time he just stood with a far-off look on his face. I thought the dusk was recalling his father to him, but he pointed out to the flats and said: "There's someone comin'."

The clouds were red over the flats and darkness was moving in. About a mile to the south something was making dust, and as we looked it showed itself to be a canvas-top wagon.

"Jimmy get over by the Indian's next to those things we gathered." This time he moved. "And put that box

35

of shells inside your shirt!" I called after him.

John Bear went inside his hut and closed the door. I put on my shirt and stood in front of the dugout, and I loosened the Colt in my belt.

We waited without moving for the wagon to arrive. It came on with a bump over the graves. When it reached the town's edge the team slowed to a walk, a six-horse team, and I wondered what kind of covered wagon needed six horses. They were well used. Slowly down the burnt-out street they came as if the driver was taking in the sight. Then they turned and pulled the creaking rig on toward me.

"Hollo!" the driver called. He reined in just as I thought he was going to ride on past. He sat up there behind his steaming horses, a stout man, smiling widely under a bushy mustache, he might have been a smith except that he wore a striped shirt with sleeve garters. Turning in his seat he said to someone inside the wagon: "See, was no prairie fire, where is grass for prairie fire?"

"Well you're a damn genius, Zar," a woman's voice came from inside, "but I don't see no Culver City neither." I saw her come up behind his shoulder and the thing that struck me was she had no bonnet on her head.

They both looked down at me.

"Frand," the man said, "there is mine camp in these hills, am I right?"

"I've heard of one," I said.

"Ah hah! I am right. And what has happened here?"

I said, "Well a man come by preaching hellfire."

He laughed and I could see the glint of a gold tooth: "Frand, listen. Two days past I learn is a mining camp westward, a place of business. But westward is big, and yesterday I am lost. Is rain, is dark, and only one strange light is in bottom of sky. You see what I'm telling you? There is good in everything, what for you was a town burning was for me a lamp in the window." The man shook as he laughed. His jowls shook, his stomach shook.

The woman said: "Don't mind Zar, he's a Russky."

"I am," the man agreed. He jumped down from the seat and I was surprised how short he was. "We make the night here, Adah, and tomorrow to the gold."

The woman disappeared in the wagon. The man said to me: "Now frand I have thirsty horses. Is that well yours?"

"That's right."

"I pay of course. You are a survivor, you will need provisions."

"Maybe."

He looked at me then as if he was hiding some joke. "You like beef? I carry beef."

As he spoke something fell off the back of the wagon and then someone jumped off and although my view was obstructed I thought it was a boy. I heard some high voices. At the same time the woman appeared at the front of the wagon and climbed down easily despite a mess of skirts.

"Adah, horses to water," the Russian said. "Others make tent in back of dugout. Like in homeland—two houses make willage."

Without unhitching the team, the woman Adah pulled them away to the water barrel. When the wagon moved off I saw three figures standing around a square bundle of canvas. This was dusk and it took me a moment to understand that they were all women. One, in pants, whom I had taken for a boy, I saw now to be a Chinese.

"You see my prize herd, frand?" the Russky poked me in the ribs and chuckled. "Water for beef, is fair?"

"Hey Zar," one woman called, "can't you wait till we've been in a place five minutes? I swear you'd trade with a cactus if you met up with one."

"Hey Zar," another called, "that little old boy yonder looks more able than the feller you talkin' to."

The Chinawoman giggled and Zar raised his fist and shouted: "Shod up!"

But I almost laughed myself. Here I was with nothing between me and the Fates but the clothes on my back, I was hard put just to stay alive, and this fellow had come in off the flats to offer me luxuries. I shook my head. I told him I would rather take vittles and maybe some of his alcohol when his camp was made.

"As you weesh," he shrugged. He was disappointed, the ladies were his stock in trade. He walked over to them, did some shouting, cuffed the Chinese girl on the ear, and before long the women were putting up their tent nearby.

Well I went about my business. Together with Jimmy I toted our property inside the dugout. I got one lamp going, I put up the stove and built a fire. We tamped the floor and spread the two blankets which belonged to the Major. All the while I was thinking of the provender to be had from this Russian. I hadn't figured past the few peas and dried apples and tins of milk we'd salvaged; and I didn't relish the idea of hunting prairie dogs. These traveling people—the more I thought about them the better I liked them.

There was a commotion just as we had things about settled. Jimmy stuck his head out of the door: "It's over by the Indian's!" he called.

I looked out. It was already dark. There were lights in front of Bear's shack, and a lot of yelling. "Stay here

Jimmy," I said and I ran over. The Russian's women were standing in the door waving their lamps and jabbering away. Inside, John Bear was lying face down on the ground. This Zar was trying to lift Molly under the arms and she was screaming and tearing at his face with her fingers.

"Here, let her be, mister!" I said. I pulled my gun out and trained it on him. He put Molly down readily enough and turned to me, but he didn't seem to notice I was covering him.

"Ah frand," he said, "you tell me what this is? My girls come to say hollo and what do they find but this savage?"

"That's right," the woman Adah said. "Sittin' on his haunches starin' at her behind. I never seen the likes!"

"Oh you sons of bitches," Molly moaned.

"That don't go where I come from," one of the women said. "No damn Indian—"

"This lady is burned," I said.

"Well alright if that's so, we can fix her up fine in the tent, we can take care of her."

"Don't you touch me!" Molly screamed. "Whores! Keep away from me!"

"Well I like that for being grateful," Adah said.

I said: "The Indian's a good doctor."

The Russian raised his bushy eyebrows: "He doctors?"

"He's been taking care of Molly."

"Wal I have killed him with my fist. On his neck I hit him."

I kneeled down for a look at Bear. He wasn't dead, he was stunned. I helped him sit up in a corner.

Molly was saying, "Blue get these whores away from me, oh Christ get them away from me!"

"Honey," one of the women said to her, "look at

you all covered with dirty redskin medicine, no
wonder you're complainin'. Now you come on with us
and Adah'll fix you up proper."

I thought Molly would have a fit. She was crying
and beating her fists on the ground: "For Godsake I'll
die if they touch me, oh God, keep them away. . . ."
But what was worse, she suddenly left off and crawled
around in the dirt until she found her little cross. She
clutched it in her hands and began to mumble to herself, her lips moved fast and her eyes began to roll
upwards.

"Ay, poor woman," Zar said fingering the scratches
on his face, "she has sharp nails for a believer."

"It's a cryin' shame," said Adah, "lyin' in the mud
that way."

I looked at John Bear, still sitting groggy in the
corner. And I looked at these righteous people crowd-
ing the shack. "Molly you'll come with me," I said.

Bending down, I lifted her arms and put her over
my shoulder. I expected her to struggle but she made
no move to stop me, she weighed like a baby. The air
was chill so I told the Russian to put the buffalo robe
over her. The minute the robe touched her, Molly
gasped and dug her nails in my neck. I carried her out
of the shack and toward the dugout, the ladies of the
brush following me with their oil lamps throwing a
jumpy glow on the ground.

When I got to the dugout I stepped past Jimmy and
laid Molly down on a blanket. Then I hung up the
other blanket for the door and poked my head out and
said to these still-chattering women: "Alright, I'll take
care of her, she'll be alright."

But when I turned back inside, Molly was looking at
her palm—she couldn't find her cross. "They took it
from me, they stole it!" she cried out. And then she

began to wail again and to curse. She cursed her father and her mother, she cursed the day she was born, she cursed herself for coming West, she cursed me. And while she ranted and carried on, Jimmy slipped out and found the cross lying on the ground halfway to the Indian's shack where she had dropped it. He came back in and went to his knees by her side and held it out with that solemn Fee look on his face.

Molly, all streaked with tears and dirt, looked up at Jimmy as if seeing him for the first time.

I was wishing she could look at me that way. I said: "Molly, you remember Fee's boy. . . . "

A FEW MINUTES LATER THEY WERE BOTH SLEEPING sound. It was warm in the dugout, we were like three creatures in a hole, and I sat down to rest a bit before I followed the Russian and his ladies to their tent. I stretched my legs and closed my eyes and I fell asleep. Now I'm trying to write what happened and I wonder, does a dream come under that? I dreamed the Man from Bodie was driving a herd across some badland; and riding each head was a wolf or some buzzard with its claws planted. I was in the middle, running with the rest, and I couldn't shake free of those claws. They drove me to my knees and I tumbled and was stomped into the earth by those behind me, dirt was filling my mouth. It was the taste of dirt woke me. Pieces of dried-out sod were falling from the wall, on my face. I got a shock because through the edge of the blanket hanging for a door I saw it was broad daylight outside. I had slept right through. Molly and Jimmy were still asleep as I crawled out and stood up stiffly, blinking in the sun.

It was well along in the afternoon and I was sure those traveling people were gone. But I turned and ten yards in back of the dugout there they were striking their tent. It was a big army tent and they were having trouble, they were too busy to do the striking—they were arguing. When one made to pull up a stake another shouted something, and then they all had to shout something. In the light I could see the women better than I had the night before: the one called Adah seemed to be older than the rest, the Chinese and the other two—one tall, one kind of dumpity—were not much more than girls.

I was happy to see them.

But this Zar caught sight of me in the middle of a long harangue and he tacked me on to the end of it: "And you, frand, are no frand of mine!" he shouted.

I didn't know what to say to that, I walked over to the well to wash off. He came up to me, talking every step of the way: "So what shall I do now? All morning I search for trail to mining camp! You did not tell me there was none, you said nothing. And now I have women who should be on their back and they are on my neck. Four days have I lost!"

My head was still filled with sleep. "Trail up through those rocks plain as day," I said.

"You call that trail? It is for ants. How can I get my wagon on that trail?"

He was right there, I hadn't understood he wanted to wagon straight up to the lodes—I should have, there was nothing else he would want to do.

"Well mister, that's just a back trail. The town you wanted is on the trade roads another two days travel from here. I guess you followed the wrong light after all."

He was mad. The veins in his neck stood out. He let go in Russian and in English and the words flew. When I bent down to pour some water over my neck he bent down too, and when I threw my head back to drink he addressed my Adam's apple. When he ran out of names to call me, he pointed to the scratches on his face and went on to Molly—a "cat woman" he called her—and when he finished with that subject he turned and stalked back to his girls.

Well I thought for sure I had lost the trade on the well water. This Russian wouldn't hand me a bean now. And if he had ridden up two days before he did or two days after, that would have been the end of it.

But my head cleared and I remembered something.

I ran after him: "Look here," I said, "if you can't get to the gold maybe the gold will come to you."

"What's this?"

"Come on Zar," the dumpity girl said, "we're wastin' time, this place gives me the chills."

"What gold?" he said, ignoring her.

I talked for all I was worth. I told him—exaggerating a little—what a thriving town this had been until two days ago. I told him how the miners came every Saturday night, a regular crowd of them, to spend money and blow off steam. I told him there was no reason they wouldn't show up just like they always did —for as I'd remembered, this was Saturday.

For a few seconds I had him. He pulled on his mustache and frowned and worried the idea some. But then he made up his mind: "No. We go." What saved me was that he and the ladies weren't in agreement which way to go. He was for striking west to the big roads, they wanted to turn back. The bunch of them

43

bickered and sulked, shouted and threatened each other while I kept glancing up to the rocks and hoping the time would be with me. Whenever it seemed as if an accord was about to be made, I put in a word that would start the arguing up all over again. Only the Chinagirl had nothing to say, she stared from one to the other, wondering how things would turn out. She was the one who first spotted the three figures on muleback looking on from high in the rocks.

"Wave, girls, wave!" Zar shouted.

And they did, jumping and waving their kerchiefs, calling "Hey! Hey!" until the miners began to ride down.

The sun was just setting. Zar snapped out orders to the girls and while they got busy preparing he took me over to his wagon and gave me a bag of flour, some strips of dried beef and a can of lard. He was smiling, I was his frand again.

But I wasted no time tucking that barter in the dug-out.

FOUR

A FEW HOURS LATER THERE WERE A GOOD dozen mules and horses roped out by the tent. Singing was coming from inside and it was a strange sound in the night air. Those miners hadn't taken but a few minutes to get over the wonder of the town ruins; one or two had put off their interest in the new whores for a few moments while they rode out to the graves to take off their hats.

But I talked with one man I knew. Angus Mcellhenny, a short old digger who kept a pipe in his teeth and had likely shot a hundred grubstakes before he gave in to work company lodes. Angus couldn't believe what had happened.

"Just one of them Blue?" he kept saying.

"Just one Angus."

"They roam in packs mostly, they like to put on fer each other."

"Well he was alone."

"My God. The doorty bastard. Say him once more."

"Well he was a big man, a head taller than me, and he had this blaze over one side of his face. But what you'd remember are his eyes. He had eyes like a spooked horse."

"Sure. I know the mon. It would be Clay Turner."

45

"He was headed your way."

"My God, likely he rode right by the camp."

"You know him?"

"I know of him. Why he should be dead, he went bad years ago." Angus took his pipe out of his mouth and spit: "I wish him in Hell, he's been ridin' too long."

There was a big laugh from the tent and the tall girl came out leading a man by his ear. He was guffawing, he was well along. Angus and I stepped out of the way as she led him around to the side of the tent and pushed him up in the covered wagon and climbed in after him.

"Blue," said Angus, "come have one with me and we'll drink to old Flo, God keep her."

It was hot enough for midnight in that tent. Kerosene lanterns were hooked to the tentpoles and they threw a yellow cast over all the smiling faces. Over on one side the Russian had a bar set up, a plank laid across two sawhorses. His sleeves were rolled and a big apron was tied around his stomach and he was drawing whiskey from a cask to fill the orders of the girls. Zar was in a sweat, his face was red, his eyes bright. On the plank right by his hand was a shotgun. And on the ground by his feet was a sack into which he dropped the silver the girls brought him, or the pouches of dust.

"On house frand," he shouted, and poured two drinks in tin cups. Angus Mcellhenny and I drank to the memory of redheaded Florence.

Some of the customers were sprawled on camp meeting chairs, some on the ground; there were those who made a point of pinching the dumpity girl or the Chinese as they went by, there were a few gathered around Adah, who was leading the singing and playing on an old melodeon.

All I need in this lifetime
Pretty girl and a silver mine...

is what they sang but the song broke up when one man
in back of Adah leaned over, put his hands in her dress
and gave her a good shake. Adah shrieked, stood up
and slapped him smart, and that made everyone laugh
including her.

Adah called to the dumpity girl: "Do your dance
Mae!"

And then all attention was fixed on Mae as she
lifted her arms above her head and began turning
around and around. The miners started to clap time
and she spun faster and faster until her skirts rose and
showed her legs above the shoes. At the height of the
dance she stopped suddenly and yanked a man to his
feet and led him right out of the tent while everyone
laughed and yelled after him. The tall girl—Jessie,
they greeted her—brushed back in a minute later and
she went directly to sit on the lap of a glaze-eyed boy
who still had his pimples. I saw the Chinagirl, dressed
in a red satin shirt and bloomers with a yellow sash
around her waist, she was on her knees offering a
drink to one grey old fellow who stared at her while he
pulled on his beard. He reached for her instead of the
whiskey but she held up her hand and smiled, I suppose she had to wait her turn for the wagon.

These girls knew how to work, they didn't pick but
the drunkest of the lot, or the least able. It looked to
me like Zar the Russian had an establishment that put
old Avery's to shame.

Angus Mcellhenny still wanted to buy me a drink
and I let him. But when he turned away and got caught
up in the revelry I took the cup and left. The song

began again and I could hear it as I walked through the
cold air to the dugout:

> *All I want before I'm old*
> *Big fat woman and a mountain of gold . . .*

In the dugout Molly and Jimmy were chewing on
strips of the dried beef like a pair of dogs, lying there
with only the light of the glowing stove, listening to the
sound of the frolic outside. It was a mournful sight. I
poked up the fire, and with our skillet and some lard I
made up a batter of flour-and-water cakes. I gave two
of the cakes to Jimmy and put two down in front of
Molly. She turned her head away.

"Molly," I said, "I have some liquor here and if you
eat those cakes you can wash them down with the liquor."

She said nothing. But at that moment I heard a
woman's voice just outside: "Not that way you old
ass!" At the same time someone stumbled against the
dugout and one of the roofboards fell inside, hitting
Molly on the back. Molly set up a yell and I picked up
the board and ran out. That dumpity girl, Mae, was
pulling her customer back to the tent while he laughed
and coughed and stumbled along.

Well I put the board back in place and I sat down
against the sod wall so I could watch and keep the
drunks away. I sat there sipping the whiskey Molly
didn't want; it was good whiskey and it warmed my
gullet, but the rest of me grew cold in that chilly air.
The windmill creaked in the darkness and one of the
horses would nicker now and then and I must have
heard twenty verses of that song rising out of the tent.
But what I listened to was the talk coming through the
sod wall at my back.

"Go ahead," it was Molly's voice, "take a look. Go on now, is it bleeding back there?"

"No."

"Alright, you're a good boy.... I knew your Pa."

"Yes."

"He liked Flo—"

"Yes."

"He's dead now, for all the good it did him."

There was no answer, but a burst of shouts and laughing came over from the tent.

"Why d'you cry!"

"I—I ain't."

"So he's dead. There's worse than that, look at me. You don't have to cry for Fee. How old are you?"

"He said twelve."

"When?"

"I don't—I don't remember."

"Twelve. Well you're small for your age. Go on and eat up that prairie cake, you want to grow into a man don't you? Oh God my back is on fire, oh Christ!... Go on and eat, little boy, I can tell you a man is hard enough to be even with proper eatin'!"

Later I fell asleep sitting there and through the night I kept waking to the shrieks of the women or the roar of the men. The light streaming from the tent fixed in a yellow square on my mind and from time to time I saw figures buck through it and disappear like phantoms beyond its edge. Toward the dawn I was aware of some mules trotting off and when the night lifted and I woke, stiff in the grey light, I could see miners sleeping all around like stones.

I got up and walked about and came on Angus Mcellhenny: he was slumped and snoring in Hausenfield's old bathtub which sat out in back of the ruins like some stranded schooner. The sight of Angus that way did not cheer me up. I felt a great melancholy looking on him in the gloom of the grey morning. What good anyone could come to on this ashen townsite I could not see.

As THE DAY CAME UP I FOUND ENOUGH TO DO: I mixed up more batter for our breakfast, I looked for a pot for Molly's use, I knocked a frame together for the door of the dugout, I gathered chips for fire from under the feet of the animals still tethered near the tent, I took the Major's pony out where there was some brush he could work on. As the sun got higher the miners began to stir, and one by one they got up cussing or groaning, and they left. I heard one man say to his mule: "Now Blossom you walk nice and easy so as old Jake's head don't topple." And another, that pimply boy, who looked sick and miserable in the daylight, came over with a crumpled letter in his hand.

"I always post my letters with Mr. Maple," he said to me.

"Well Ezra's gone," I said.

"Alright, you can hold my letter for the stage." He brought two cartwheels out of his pocket and put them in my hand. "It's two dollars the ounce and I never say more than an ounce's worth."

He was off before I could say yes or no, and I think it was this as much as anything which caused things to go as they did. Zar the Russian was climbing down from his wagon with a whistle on his lips when he saw the boy give me the letter and ride off. He buttoned his shirt and called to me. Together we built up a fire and he brewed some real coffee and gave me a mug.

Then, sitting on the ground, he asked me to tell him what, truly, had happened to the town. I told him.

"So," he said, "was a sudden man."

"That's right."

He pointed to the boy's letter which I had put in my shirt pocket: "And town is gone but use for town may not be gone. Am I right?"

"You're right."

"And will stage come again?"

"I reckon. If it pays."

"Will come stage again. Will come miners again!" He couldn't contain himself at the idea, he jumped up and began pacing and pulling his beard, a round barrel of a man muttering to himself in Russian. I drank the hot coffee and watched him. He stopped to look around: he looked at the windmill, he looked at the rock hills, he turned a full circle, looking east over the rubble of the burnt-out street and looking south over the flats to the horizon. The sun was at noon and it bleached the flats almost white with shimmers of yellow or pale green where the ground dipped or lay in the shadow of a cloud.

"Frand," he said taking a deep breath, "what do you smell?" He looked at me: "You smell the coffee? You smell the horse? You smell the burn in the air?"

I nodded. "Ah, you have not the merchant's nose. You know what I smell? The money!" He looked at me and that gold tooth showed out through his beard and he was laughing hard, holding his hands on his sides and shaking fit to bust. He laughed so loud that Jimmy came out of the dugout to see.

"You unnerstand what I'm telling you, frand," Zar said. "We shall be neighbors here!" He leaned over and slapped me on the shoulder. Still laughing he walked quickly over to the tent and went inside.

Well his coffeepot was still on the fire so I filled my cup again and motioned for Jimmy to come over.

"Drink this up Jimmy," I said. He took the coffee without a word. I noticed he looked better with a good night's sleep in back of him, those Fee eyes were not so deep in his head.

"Is Molly still asleep?"

"No. She's saying words."

"What?"

"She's saying words to herself. With that cross."

"Is she praying?"

"Yes, she's praying."

When he finished I filled the cup again. "Take this to her," I said, "she'll take it from you. Maybe a cup of coffee is what she's praying for."

Walking carefully Jimmy went toward the dugout. But then some loud protest caterwauled from the tent and he stopped for a moment and looked back at me.

"Go ahead," I called, "that's just those people."

I put more water in the Russian's coffeepot and set it back on the fire. Then I stood listening to the awful sounds from the tent. The ladies were sleeping in there and Zar had gone in to tell them they were going to be founders of a new town. It was a furious racket. I could hear him shout and I could hear them shout back. I figured the only one not putting up a squawk was the Chinese, and I was right. In a few minutes she pushed the flap aside and came out limping a little, to stare at the rocks and the flats and the ruins.

I had an idea at that moment. I went over to the bathtub and rolled Angus out on the ground. He didn't even miss a snore. I dragged the tub back to the well, washed it out as best I could, and filled it with pails of water. I could see the sun shaking in that water and it showed back the blue sky. Given time to warm in the day's heat it would be an inviting thing; I have my share of cunning.

As I waited the argument inside the tent fell off until I could hear only one of the women standing up to Zar's tirades. She appeared outside and it was the plump one, Mae. Mae stalked over to the wagon and climbed in and started to throw things over the side. A pot, a blanket, a carpetbag. "I ain't goin' to, no sir," she was yelling, "y'all can fry here in this hole for all I care!"

Zar had followed her and he was standing by waving his fist: "You think you are too good for this place! You think you know better than Zar what to do! I will kill you with my hands, Maechka!"

For answer she threw out an oval looking glass and it caught him square on the side of the head. I could have laughed but the Russian roared with rage. Jumping up on the wagon he stuck his arm inside and pulled the woman out and threw her to the ground.

"Hey Zar!" the tall one, Jessie, called. "None of that!" She and Adah were standing in front of the tent, red-eyed, watching the battle. In the bright daylight and rumpled with sleep, none of the women looked too good. Their face paint was rubbed off and their hair was hanging and they all looked the worse for wear.

"I say what we do, no one else!" Zar was shouting. And to make his point he was kicking Mae as she tried to get up. When she got to her feet and tried to run he knocked her down and kicked her again. She was screaming and he was saying, "You will shod up, shod up!"

I ran over and pulled him away from the girl, she had given up trying to get away and was just lying there curled up and crying with her head between her arms. Zar let me lead him away but he turned every few steps to curse her in Russian.

The Chinagirl had run inside the tent when Zar came out but Jessie and Adah went over to Mae and helped her up. Adah put her arm around the bruised girl and mothered her. Witnessing this I was ashamed of myself. But I left Zar sitting crosslegged and surly by his cooking fire and I went over to the unhappy women and allowed they could use the bathtub by the well if they liked.

They must not have seen a tub in months. Mae forgot her peeve in a moment and she and Jessie stripped themselves clear down to their hides and took turns sitting in the tub, splashing and laughing like children. They rubbed themselves with a piece of scented soap which Adah brought out to them. "It's genuine Parisiun!" Adah called to me. "Got it from some son of a bitch what stole it from a Colonel's lady!"

The Chinese stood off a ways just looking on, and she was smiling with delight. Those two jumping in and out of the tub, red down to their necks and up to their wrists but white everywhere else, were as mindful of anyone watching as if they had been whole dressed. One watcher was Jimmy, standing against the dugout, and I couldn't tell him not to, I was another.

THAT EVENING I SAT AT THE RUSSIAN'S FIRE AND I told him it would be a good idea to put up some tolerable buildings before the stage came. I remembered that Fee bought some of his wood from the mines but that most of it he garnered from dead towns in the territory.

"So let us find such a town," Zar said.

"Well there's one I know of," I said, "name of Fountain Creek."

"Good. We go now." He stood up. This fellow had a better mind than Avery ever had but it would outrun you with your own intentions. I used to own a horse like that, you spurred him once and you couldn't hold him.

"Wait on," I said, "it's a half day's travel. You don't gain anything losing a night's sleep. We'll head out at sunup."

But once it was decided I began to worry the whole idea. It was all too quick for me; glad as I was to be staking out in earnest I couldn't believe in it altogether, almost against my will I found myself glancing up at the shadows of the rocks. I didn't like leaving Molly and the boy untended for a day and maybe a night too.

Well I was up and waiting for the dawn. When the first light ran through the sky I went over to the Indian's shanty. As I feared, John Bear was in no humor to keep a watch out for anyone, he had not come out of his shack since Zar had knocked him down; and I saw him through the door sitting hunched up in front of a dead fire, he was deep in a brood. There isn't much worse you can do to an Indian than touch him. Bear wore a shirt and britches and he was living in this shack where ten years before he wouldn't have sat down under a roof—but for all he felt now he might just as well have stayed a blanket Indian.

In the chilly early morning Zar had unloaded his wagon and now he was stripping it down, pulling off the canvas and lifting the struts away. On the ground were trunks, sacks of grain, boxes, a barrel, bedding —he packed a lot in that wagon. The women were up and about, laboring to get it all inside the tent.

"I am soon ready, frand," he called. I went over to him and told him Bear was in the dumps. He wasn't too concerned, he said: "The savage will get over it." I remember those words.

"Well that may be," I said, "but meanwhile there's no one to keep an eye out while we're gone."

"So?" He shrugged. I didn't know what to do, I didn't want to leave—especially with Molly in the dugout the way she was. But there seemed to be no way out of it. I finally asked around till the tall girl, Jessie, said she had an old dress she might be willing to sell. I offered her the two dollars that pimply boy had given me to post his letter.

"No," she said, changing her mind, "it's too good for Madam Bitch in there."

"Give it him," Zar said, scowling.

So the exchange was made and I took the frock in to Molly. She was sitting up facing the doorway and she was holding the buffalo robe to her shoulders. Those green eyes in that peaked face made me feel again the queerness, the dismal shame of trying to speak to her. I had to clear my throat.

"Molly, things are going good, these people want to stake out here. I'm going off with the Russian to find a load of wood for building."

She nodded, she didn't seem to care.

"Jimmy'll stay behind," I said. "And this is a dress."

It was to plague me for a long time, like this, that I couldn't tell what she would answer or if I might find a moment's favor in her eyes. She didn't say anything till I began to wonder if she'd heard me; and then I saw she was crying, not making a sound, just looking at the ground as if her whole life was laid out in front of her, while the tears ran down her face.

"Molly, it's a proper dress," I said. But she wouldn't take it. "Wear it yourself, Mayor." She sat there biting her lips and running her hand through her hair. I didn't know what to answer, so I went back outside with the dress.

Jessie saw me and by the time I reached the tent she and Adah and Mae had stopped what they were doing to gather around me.

"I knew it," Jessie said, "why she suckles bobcats, she'd do it with a horse, that bitch, the dress is too good for her."

"I'll be damned," Adah said.

"How do you like that Lady Bacon Ass," Jessie said to Mae, "that's somethin' ain't it?"

"Trouble with that ol' girl," Mae said slowly, "she were burned not hardly enough."

I was scratching the stubble on my chin; and listening to these women made me say something I don't understand to this day. Maybe I wanted to keep Molly from their scorn; maybe it was just some mournful deviltry in me.

"Molly's my wife," I said. I think I was just saying what I knew, that we had been wedded by the Bad Man from Bodie.

Well they looked at me as like struck dumb. I saw a doubt in Jessie's eye—she may have wondered why I'd left my wife to lie in an Indian's shack where they found her—but it was gone in a second. I suppose there is nothing that a whore will respect more than a married woman. Those ladies stammered and blushed like virgins, and the next thing I knew Adah had taken me inside the tent, opened her trunk and dug something up from the bottom of it.

"This here's my wedding dress," she said to me, "I wore it once only, on my marriage day. Twenty years ago. My husband was a minister. This was his tent, those were his meetin' chairs, that was his melodeon and I played the hymns for him. I don't have a ring on m'finger 'cause I'm ashamed to wear it, but you can tell her this dress is clean."

"Well now Miss Adah—"

"Go on, you take it." She folded this white dress over my arm. "It's simple, it will do her fine, poor woman, gettin' burned that way it's no wonder she ain't herself."

"That's right," said Jessie.

"And give him his two dollars Jessie," Mae said.

"That's right," Jessie said and she put the money back into my hand. "Gimme that old dress, it ain't fit, I ought to bury it."

"Ladies," I said, "you are awful kind." I was doing alright for a liar, but I meant what I said; it should have saddened me how kind they suddenly were except I knew what they might have done to Molly if they'd found she was one of their kind.

When I stepped out of the tent Zar was up on his wagon and his team was in place: "Wal frand," he called, "I wait."

"Hold on a minute," I said. I found Jimmy around at the front of the dugout. He had been up and about for just a few minutes and the sleep was still in his eyes. He was using his fingers to comb the tail of the Major's pony.

"Jimmy," I said, "listen to me careful. I'm riding out now to scare up some wood. I want you to give this dress to Molly after I leave. She needs some covering and she'll take it if you give it to her. While I'm gone I want you to keep the pony hitched to the rig and right by here. If you see any sign of that Bad Man take Molly and light out south to the wagon trails. Do you understand me?"

"Yes."

"You shouldn't have any trouble. Just don't stray,

stay close by. Don't bother the Indian, he's in the dumps, he might be mean. Eat up those prairie cakes I made. Probably those ladies'll give you some hardtack if you ask them. Alright?"

"Yes."

"I'll be back." I started off and then I turned back: "If someone asks you how your Ma is feeling, they'll mean Molly."

A minute later I was up on the box beside the Russian; he snapped his whip and we skidded off with a clatter. I turned in my seat to look back: no one watched us go but Jimmy; he stood by the dugout staring after us, and as we drew further away and I looked back again he still stood there without moving. I wished I had said something to make him feel better, or maybe tousled his head.

The Russian drove his horses as if he was racing a train, I had to grab the box while the empty wagon swung out one way and then another behind the team. I pointed south and west across the flats and that's the way we went, rumbling, bumping through the stumped-up dust. It was no situation for any kind of talk but the Russian didn't know it. He was one of those people proud of himself and his station in life and he shouted out his story as we rolled on under the sun, and he kept up even after the flats gave way to fixed swells of sand, sparsely weeded, that stretched on ahead of the eye like a solid sea. I only half listened, I was thinking of Molly and would she wear that dress. "Frand...I come West to farm...but soon I learn, I see...farmers starve...only people who sell farmers their land, their fence, their seed, their tools ...only these people are rich. And is that way with everything...not miners have gold but salesmen of burros and picks and pans...not cowboys have money but saloons who sell to them their drinks, gamblers who play with them faro . . . not those who look for money but those who supply those to look. These make the money . . . So I sell my farm . . . and I think . . . what need is there I shall fill it . . . and I think more than picks and pans, more than seed, more even than whiskey or cards is need for Women. And then I meet widow Adah, owner of tent . . . And I am in business."

W<small>E REACHED FOUNTAIN CREEK AT NOON. IT</small> stood in some tall yellow grass by the banks of a dried-out arroyo, a deserted street of shackly buildings, corrals rotted by the weather, porches grown over with weeds. Before we got to work we took some pulls on the Russian's water bottle and ate some tack he had brought. Rusted tin cans were lying all over, half buried in sand, the hot pebbly wind was swinging the door of a roofless hut at the far end of the street. I spotted a mangy slant-eyed wolf crouched under a porch not fifty feet from where we were. He was watching us close.

"He's a hungry one," I said to Zar, "he'll go for these horses if we let him."

"So, we won't let him." Still chewing a mouthful, Zar reached for his shotgun and slowly brought it around and shot off both barrels at the wolf. The animal was out of there fairly, along with his mate that we hadn't seen, and the two of them bounded away along the arroyo.

"Their courage'll be back by and by," I said, "let's get to work."

We went for the corrals first, untying what rawhide lashes we could, cutting the rest, laying the poles down lengthwise on the wagon bed. Then we began collecting lumber from the frame houses and barns, staying away from places where the white ants were too thick, prying off boards, knocking away doors, pulling up porch planks, shakes, beams, shingles. There was so much rot in everything it was a wonder the buildings were upright at all. We worked all through the afternoon hardly stopping for a drink, coughing with the dust that rose, the sand blown by the wind. Our friends the wolves had cut down the mice and burrowing owls to be found but bugs and spiders scuttled away from our axe and pick. We worked till we judged the wagon could hold no more, the wood was stacked a tall man's height above the driver's box. Then we went around picking up every nail in sight. And we came on a set of bright white human bones sitting in the arroyo. We stood looking at that skeleton. It was clean. I had to think what an indecency it is that leaves only the bones to tell what a man has been.

"Fountain Creek," Zar said. He was mopping his neck with his handkerchief. "Frand, you see the peril. Always the ghost city is one with name full of promise. Is that not so? We must have care in our naming not to make this mistake. . . ."

It was dark when we were ready to leave. I took the reins and the Russian sat atop the lumber to weight it. The horses strained to get the wheels turning and we moved off at a walk. I'll tell you I was weary on that trip: the night was black with stars and the wagon creaked and swayed and I slipped in and out of dreaming. I couldn't believe the horses had a destination, I kept thinking I was traveling to no purpose. What good was this to that woman and that boy? What could I hope to do for them? Only a fool would call anywhere in this land a *place* and everywhere else a journey to it.

I must have fallen asleep and the horses must have stopped—because I awoke to the boom of the Russian's shotgun and the wagon lurched forward and the reins went taut in my hands. There was a light in the sky ahead of us.

"Those damn wolves have been following," Zar called down, "but they are running now!"

Later we rode up to the town and Jimmy came running out to meet us. "A man's here with that same wagon," he said, "the one they put my Pa in—"

He was about to cry. I got down, stiff, and took his hand: "Say what Jimmy? What, boy?"

"Over there." Standing by the well was Hausenfield's hearse. I didn't trust my eyes, I went over for a close look. There was the mule and the grey; the pick was still wedged across the black door. And a skinny, chinless fellow with a leather vest was leaning against a wheel, looking at me sly.

"Howdo."

"Where did you find this wagon?" I said.

"Hit waer jes setting out thaer. I tuk it up."

"And you've not looked in the door?"

"Didn't think to—"

"Well that's alright," I said, "this is a burying wagon, you ever do any burying?"

"Never have."

"Well you'll find your first customer inside."

Then I turned and saw Molly holding herself up at the side of the dugout. She had on that white dress and she was smiling at me, a queer bitter smile. I rubbed my hand across my eyes and I thought why I have a safe name for this town, we'll call it Hard Times. Same as we always called it.

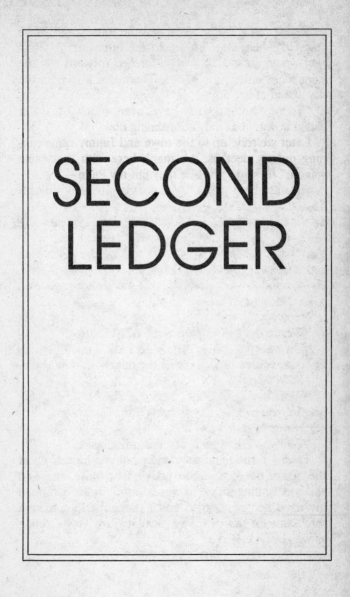

SECOND
LEDGER

FIVE

THAT WAS THE WAY IT ENDED AND BEGAN AGAIN. From the day I returned Molly wore the wedding dress like she was born to it, she walked stiffly with her shoulders thrown back and her mouth grim against the pain. And when the pain was gone the set of it remained, the healed burns pulled her up tight, her chin was always in the air and the chain and cross was always plain to see around her neck. So that whenever I looked at her I was looking at rebuke.

The day Zar and I started to put up our buildings Molly took John Bear's buffalo robe out of the dugout and went to return it to the Indian. Over to his shack she marched, stirred him out of the dumps and gave him back the lice-ridden fur with what must have been proud apology. I could see by her manner when she came back, it was as if the Indian's property had been stolen by some no-account thief and she had squared the scales by returning it.

Molly was plentiful in her moods, unspeaking for days at a time, smiling with plans maybe or weeping for no clear reason but her memories. But when she had a mind to she could make anything in the world seem a taint on me. One morning Jimmy was helping me mix up some sod for chinking. Mae, the dumpity girl, came by with nothing much on her mind and started to talk to the boy and tease him a bit. Jimmy always watched Zar's women with great attention and that gave them pleasure.

"Y'all sweet on me, li'l ol' Jimmy?" the girl asked.

He blushed.

"Ya'all take a fancy to Mae, don't yuh?"

"No ma'am."

"Here put yo' hand here, now ain't that soft as soft?"

She was holding Jimmy's hand on her bosom and that's when Molly showed up to give her a cuff on the ear. Mae was so shocked she had no anger but just bit her lip and ran off; Jimmy was suddenly back to the sod; and Molly stood regarding me as she would a lizard.

It was no pain I felt but a steady ache, like some hand was gently squeezing my heart. It never left me. I would look out to the graves in the flats or look up to the rocks or over at the scar of the old street and always I saw the face of the Man from Bodie. That was the trouble, I know now, that was my failing, that I couldn't see past my own feelings, I had no thoughts beyond myself. The day came when I had a sturdy clapboard cabin affixed to the dugout so that altogether we had two rooms to live in. I knocked together a table using pieces of the balustrade from the old Silver Sun, and some boards, and Jimmy and I fell into the habit of saving whatever food we had for that table each evening. Molly would serve it up and then take her portion and step down into the dugout to eat alone, leaving the boy and me to taste what sweetness we could while not looking into each other's eyes.

There was the business with Jenks. It was Jenks who brought Hausenfield's wagon in off the plains, so pleased with his booty that he hadn't smelled Hausenfield inside. His head was not much thicker than a broom handle and he had no chin to speak of; the way his sly yellowed eyes looked at you made you think of a wolf's cunning, but really he was a stupid man. Before he managed to bury the German I had to show him where to do it and to point out how he could turn up the ground with the pickaxe lying across the door, and I had to tell him how deep he'd best dig and finally I ended up doing as much as he did. Then, with Hausenfield laid away this Jenks didn't do another thing for a week but just sat around in the shade of his new wagon, eyeing the ladies or oiling his gun and his gunbelt.

Well he looked so deliberate toying with those arms day after day it took me some time to understand he was trying all the while to make up his mind for staying or moving on. He was just a poky, traveling where the trail took him, he had himself a black coach and he didn't know how best to gain from it. Zar was angry because I let the fellow draw free water for the mule and grey and for his own horse, a patch-bald sorrel, while he did nothing in exchange. And I began to be tried too. We neither of us figured there was much good in Leo Jenks.

But one morning Molly approached him and with a loud, throaty voice, said to him: "Mr. Jenks, you find any use for that gun except in oiling it?"

He was sitting with his back to a wheel and he sprang up fast when she spoke and took his hat off.

"Well yes'm, ah kin shoot whur yew kin see."

"Is that right?"

"It is, yes'm."

"Well I see a windmill over there, and on top of that windmill is eight stubby blades and I'm looking at the one wavin' straight up at heaven."

67

Jenks put on his hat and cocked his pistol, aimed, and sent off a shot which splintered the topmost blade. The horses shied. Over by his shack John Bear stopped hoeing his rows and stood up to watch.

"I see the neck of a bottle," cried Molly, "sticking up out of that rubble there."

Jenks turned, took aim where she pointed, and the piece of glass sprayed into the air. Three more times Molly fixed her eye on things—a stone, a hump of dirt, a stick of wood—and each time this Jenks placed his round where she called it. The shots echoed off the rock hills and came back to us. Everyone was watching now, the women over by their tent, Zar from a corner of his new corral, and Jimmy squatting on the back of the Major's buckboard. I was close enough to Jenks to see that when he took his aim those shifty wolf eyes of his squinted with some true knowledge.

He finally holstered his pistol and took his hat off again.

"I thank you, Mr. Jenks," Molly said looking my way, "it's good to find a man in these parts. I wish the Lord my husband knew the gun the way you do!"

After that Jenks had no trouble deciding what was his aim in life. He rode the wagon off east one dawn and at night came back with a half a dozen prairie dogs slung from the box. You have to be quick to hit a prairie dog while he's diving for his hole—I learned later Jenks parked the stage in the middle of a dog town and lay atop of it for hours till the animals forgot he was there and came up out of their burrows.

Jenks turned out to be a good hunter and he bartered his kills for my water or for Zar's liquor or for one of the girls. Fresh meat is a luxury and there is nothing will go down easier than a well-roasted haunch of dog or a good rabbit stew. But when Molly cooked up some of Jenks's meat she always spiced it with her scorn, which made it hard to swallow.

B<small>Y THE TIME THE STAGE CAME WE WERE SEEING</small> the last of summer. The sun was getting white and it was setting earlier. The winds were lasting and they put out more of a bite. Each day they blew off more of the old town dust and ate away the char of the old street. Zar had his place built, a long low public house of clapboard and sod, it stood where his tent had stood—on the north side of the windmill—and its door, like the door of my new shack, faced to the southeast. When the stage drove in it was in front of Zar's that the driver reined his horses.

We were all there to meet it, even John Bear. The stage was run by the Territory Express Company and the name was painted in red letters along the side. The letters were well covered with dust and grime, the tails of the horses were caked with mudballs. Our town was a good trip from the last stop.

The driver was Alf Moffet; I knew him. He sat up on his box leaning forward with his arms on his knees and the reins loose in his hand. He was looking for a face he knew and the first one he saw was Molly.

"Why Miss Molly," he said, "I heard you and Flo was dead."

Molly frowned but she said nothing. The Russian and his ladies were right there and I feared Alf would say too much. I had not had trouble with any of the miners that way. Molly was hid the first few Saturdays they came and after that they did not think to question her. But I knew Alf for a fun-loving man, he had a voice full of gravel and he liked to talk.

"Well Alf," I said stepping up and clearing my throat, "we had a fire here as you can see but we're not all dead. These here are some of our new citizens" —I pointed to Mae and Jessie and Adah—"and if you'll step down and come into the new saloon I'll buy you a drink and maybe introduce you to them."

"I can't be stopping long, Blue," Alf said, but he allowed me to take his arm while he jumped down. He grabbed his mail pouch and told the other man on the box, an old man I did not know, to unload. There were two barrels lashed to the back of the stage and a pile of boxes on the roof as well as what was inside. The Express took on freight if there was any room left after passengers. We always got supplies in plenty when it came and I had been counting on that since the day of the fire.

Inside Zar's place there were lamps burning. It was afternoon but the Russian had not built any windows. I sat Alf down on a camp chair at a wooden table and after our eyes were accustomed to the shadow I motioned to Zar and he smilingly brought over a full bottle of whiskey and two glasses—just the way I had told him to do it. The glassware was Avery's old stock Jimmy and I had recovered the day after the fire. I wanted to be careful with Alf.

He was a big square-faced man, grey underneath his hat. He tossed off three drinks neat and when the dust was washed from his throat we began talking.

"We got some orders to put in with you Alf," I said.

"Well Blue I don't know. Company wants me to tell 'em when I get back if'n Hard Times is worth the trip any more."

"Miners are showing up more than ever, Alf. The

Russian here is doing a good trade. People comin' every day. This Mr. Jenks—I don't know whether you saw him out there—he's all the way from Kentucky."

Alf tilted his head to one side and smiled at me.

"That was just a little accident, that fire," I said. "The town will be up like a weed before you know it Alf."

"Well now Blue I always liked you, yessir. If you was hanging by your fingers from a cliff you'd call it climbin' a mountain."

Alf had heard about the fire from one of the people from the town—he didn't say who. I couldn't tell him any lies. "Same thing happened just a few years back to the town of Kingsville, Kingsville, Kansas. Did you know it?"

"Never heard of it."

Alf poured another drink: "Well sir it was a good town, a railroad head. They had two, three livery stables, couple of stores, lots of nice frame houses, a jail made of brick, some dandy saloons and a two-story hotel. Bunch of these Bad Men come along one spring, stayed three days. Killed twenty people. Broke up the hotel, wrecked the stores. Bricked up the doors and windows of the jailhouse, made of it an oven and roasted the Sheriff alive. Town never came back."

"What about the railroad?"

"Catcher come along the following summer and they laid track right on through for another thirty miles. Pass by today you can wave at the prairie grass."

"Them Bad Men are sure a plague, Alf. It's no use denying. Let's have another drink."

When his head went back to receive the liquor I motioned to Zar who had been standing by the door. A moment later Mae and Jessie came in and sat down

71

at the table. After I made the introduction I went out into the light.

Bear was helping the old man unload the back of the wagon. Jimmy was on top of the stage untying the lashings. Jenks was fingering the rifle sticking out of the boot by the driver's seat. But what made me really stand up was the sight of Ezra Maple. I hadn't stopped to look for passengers, I couldn't believe my eyes. He was standing there in an Eastern suit, a carpetbag was on the ground beside him. Lord if it wasn't him!

"Ezra!" I called.

But Molly was talking to him and as I walked up she said: "Mister I told you he ain't here, he couldn't take the climate. Blue," Molly said to me, "this is Ezra Maple's brother Isaac. He's a doubtin' man, he's looking all around for the General Store."

Of course, looking closer I saw it couldn't have been Ezra: this fellow wasn't as tall, nor did he have as much of a stoop in his shoulders. He was younger, fairer-skinned. But he had that same sad-eyed long beagle's face. "Well you sure fooled me," I said. Molly went off with a short laugh and I took the man for a walk over to the spot where Ezra's store had been. I told him what had happened.

He shook his head and looked at the ground: "He shouldn't a run off knowin' I was comin'—it ain't like Ezra. Wrote a letter to him six months ago. Wrote it down plain as day!"

"Well now, Mr. Maple once a letter is west of the States it might light down anywhere. I never saw Ezra get a letter, likely it never even reached him."

He took a big curved pipe from his pocket, filled it and lighted it with a box match. He puffed and frowned and stared at the dusty rubble and shook his head: "It don't seem right at all."

I could understand his feelings. A man doesn't go West for nothing. He'd been traveling four or five weeks, by train, by steamer, by stage, thinking all the while to find his brother when he got here. And probably to make a life.

"'Come along when ye can.' Those were his words to me when he left."

"That so?"

"'Come along when ye can, there's room out there fer two.'"

"That's true enough."

"I wrote out a letter when Ma died sayin' I had only to sell the store and then I'd come. Jes the pair of us, seemed like we ought to try our fortune together. And now here I be"—he took a good look around—"and Ezra ain't, and it's a bad bargain I made."

"Well now, Mr. Maple I don't know. The water don't flow from the rocks and the game don't nibble at your back door. But the place has what they call possibilities."

He gave me a sharp, trader's look. "Well I haven't seen a tree in seven days."

"That's what they mean: look at all the possible trees could grow if they'd a mind to."

He didn't laugh but I had his attention away from Ezra for the moment. I walked him back to the well.

"I'd like you to taste this water," I said. "It's as good as any and better than most. Dip into that pail and refresh yourself. Help you to think clear on what to do."

At that moment I had no plan in my mind. But when I walked over to the stage and looked at the freight standing on the ground I had some forward-thinking thoughts. These were the store supplies Ezra Maple had ordered. There was a barrel of flour, a bar-

73

rel of beef in brine, sacks of coffee, cartons of tinned sardines, crackers—a whole lot of stuff.

Molly came up at my back: "Mayor," she said softly, "I know what you're fixing to do, but I'll tell you we don't need another Ezra Maple here. Let this man go look for his brother and may he find him in Hell."

I said nothing but went back to Zar's. Alf's hat was on the table. Mae was sitting on his lap and Jessie was standing in back of him holding his ears, and they all three were laughing.

"Blue!" Alf called throwing his head back. "I begin to see your way of thinkin', there sure is a spirit of life hereabouts, yes sir, a spirit of life!"

"Alright then Alf supposing we talk business."

Zar brought over a lamp and put it on the table. Alf excused himself to the ladies and while they stood watching he took some bills out of his pouch and spread them on the table. They were bills of transit for the goods outside and they were all marked paid.

"It adds to forty dollars Blue."

"Bot the stamp is there," Zar said examining the bills, "these goods are already paid. He wants us to pay again!"

"Tha's right," said Alf. "This provender was for Ezra Maple and Ezra ain't here. Course if you like I'll load it back on and be on my way."

"Zar," I said, "it's a fair price for the goods received. Alf here drives the best stage this side of the Platte, he's thought of highly by the Territory Express. They listen to what he says." In my own mind I had expected Alf to ask for more than forty dollars; and that he put his demands in the form he did I found to be a mark of manners. He could always have charged separate for the supplies.

"I'll give you my hand on it, Alf," I said, and we shook across the table.

Then we exchanged letters: I gave him two—the pimply boy's and another I had taken since—along with four dollars. Alf gave me one letter. "It's meant for Ezra," he said, "nail it up somewhere if he ever comes back."

Then Alf had the idea that I would like to handle the Express business for the town. I allowed I would. He gave me a printed pad for writing all orders and tickets and the terms were three percentages on all monies I garnered excepting mail. We shook on that, too, and then I left Alf to enjoy the women while I went back outside to find forty dollars.

Zar followed me: "What kind of business is that? Women we give him and whiskey and we must pay for goods already paid!"

I said: "You want him to come back don't you? We got to stay on the Company's route or all the miners on the mountain won't do us any good."

"Forty dollars!"

In the daylight I was looking at the letter Alf had given me for Ezra Maple—and it was the one Isaac himself had written from Vermont.

"Maybe it won't be your forty dollars," I said to Zar.

I walked over to the well and held out the letter to Maple, saying: "It was right along with you on the stage."

I remember he stared at that letter for a long time. He bit down on his pipe and his face got redder and redder. He was angry but there was a confusion of feeling in his face, I could tell he was glad because his brother had not run off knowing he was coming.

"What are you going to do now?" I said to him.

"Don't know. Look for Ezra. I s'pose. Hunt him up."

I did some powerful talking then. I told Isaac Maple he could go looking for his brother on a thousand different trails and he still might miss him. I told him there were mountains one way and deserts another, high enough and wide enough for armies to lose themselves in. I told him a man could use up all his money and most of his life looking for something in the West. But, I said, if he were to stake out in one place, make his name in the country, the word would travel surer than any letter that Isaac Maple was keeping a store in Hard Times. And one day the word would reach Ezra and he'd know where to come.

"Mr. Maple," I said taking him by the arm, "those goods standing on the ground over there were meant for Ezra's store. You can buy them from Alf Moffet for forty dollars. And you can sell them to the rest of us for twice that amount in water and shelter and cash together. We've a need for a store and no doubt the need will grow as more people settle here."

I talked to the man for the best part of an hour; and at the end of that time, with all of us in a circle around him, he reached in his money belt and counted out forty dollars in greenbacks, licking his thumb and feeling the texture of each bill before he gave it into my hand.

Well the minute he did that I had Zar step up and meet him, and Miss Adah, who shook his hand and made him blush, and Jenks, who nodded and blinked his wolfy eyes, and the Chinese girl and Jimmy. Bear had gone back to his shack and Molly stood straight by the door of the cabin and would not come over. But it was a proper welcome Isaac Maple got even so.

A few minutes later the tall girl, Jessie, came out of Zar's place smoothing down her hair. Then Mae followed supporting Alf who was laughing and blinking in the light. Alf had consumed a good amount of whiskey, he looked us all over standing around the stage and said: "Yessir, the spirit o' life, spirit o' life, yessir."

The old man on the box moved over to the driver's side and took up the reins and we helped Alf to sit up next to him. I gave Alf the forty dollars and the ordering list I had worked up for Zar and Isaac which he stuck in his vest.

"See you again Alf?"

"Tha's right Blue, tha's right!" He lifted his hat and his head went back as the old man flung his whip out and the wheels spun up dirt.

I felt pretty fair watching that wagon line out its dust over the flats—like I had done a good day's work. But in the evening, over our supper of salted beef newly bought from Isaac Maple's barrel, Molly couldn't see I had done anything to be satisfied of.

"We'll have to pay for this meat ten times what we could have by buying it ourselves," she said.

"Well Molly I don't favor keeping a store. Settling Ezra's brother here puts money in the town."

She looked at me. "The town! Oh Mayor you don't fool me one bit—"

"What?"

"You'll rope in every damn fool you can just to make up a herd. There's surety in numbers, ain't that what you think?"

"I don't think that."

"I know you Blue," she giggled, and Jimmy watching her laughed too. But then Molly's face went cold and she gazed at me: "Mayor, all the soft yellow spines

77

in the world stack up to nothing when the Bad Man comes. I'll tell you that, I know it."

AFTER THAT IT WAS A RACE AGAINST THE weather. Jenks began to build something with what lumber he could reclaim from the old street and it was clear to me whatever it was he was having a bad time. He finally admitted he wanted to raise a barn for his wagon and three animals. When Zar and I heard that we told him we would fetch wood from Fountain Creek and help him build a good enough stable if he would put up our horses without charge. He agreed, and we made two trips with both wagons—Zar's and the black stage—and we weren't choosy about the wood. I thought we could use every hand we had to advantage, it was a lot of work what with stalls and all; but Isaac Maple, who had rented Zar's big tent for his own shelter, had no horse of his own and he saw no reason to join in; and Bear the Indian would have nothing to do with any of this while Zar was in our company—he spent most of his time away in the rocks, preparing traps I suppose and bringing down all the brush he could find.

All during these days Jimmy worked close by me in everything. He took care of the pony, he cut roots and gathered manure for fire, he cleaned the stove and helped with the chinking of the barn walls. He was always at my side and heeding whatever I told him to do. But I remember the way he watched her when Molly one morning went over to the old street and poked around in the rubble till she found the stiletto she had dropped the day of the fire and came back to nail it, teary-eyed, above our door.

And each morning the sun came up weaker and whiter, like an old man rising from his bed, and each morning's chill was slower giving up the ground. Till finally I stood one day with the sun at its height and there was no warmth at all, but a shuddering breeze running down the neck and up the legs and lifting the clothes from the body. The winds were light but they brazed the flats with their cool blow and we hadn't much time till winter.

SIX

THE STABLE WAS NOT ROOFED BEFORE THE TRUE cold came, we drove the horses into the enclosure of the four high walls and while they snorted so you could see their breath and turned from one corner to another we took the corral apart and got some of the shaven logs up for joists. There was no good way of keeping warm except by moving. When the roof was up tolerably we made a railing of the remaining corral poles to go along in front of all the buildings—from the doors of the stable past Isaac Maple's tent and past Zar's place and the windmill to the door of the cabin I had built for Molly and Jimmy and me. A Dakota blizzard will freeze your eyes shut and drive you from your direction faster than your senses realize. I have known men to die in a drift a few feet from their doors because they had no rail to go by.

All during this hurried-up preparation against the winter I kept thinking how much we could use a good carpenter like Fee. A skilled man like that and it would not matter so much that the nails we had were soft and the lumber rotten. I worried what a blizzard might do to the stable roof. I took down the blades of the windmill to keep the water in the ground. Winter is a worrying time, you have to tuck your chin in and burrow down somewhere and hope there will still be something when the spring comes.

I had no clothes but the ones I wore, Molly had only her white dress and Jimmy had not even a hat. His pants didn't cover his ankles and I had to tie a bit of rawhide around one of his shoes to keep the sole from flapping. We were not fit to meet the winter out of doors, and I knew when it set in in earnest we would have just our roof and each other to keep us from freezing. And that would be no comfort in a real blow.

For one week running the sun didn't show through at all, the skies filled up grey and then snow began to sweep in on the wind. If you stood the bite long enough to take a look there was no more line between earth and sky. The flats were grey, the rock hills were grey and the wind, thick with snow, flew around your face in gusts so that you could even doubt your own balance, you could not be sure you were standing on ground or rising, without breath, in the sky.

The cabin I had built onto the dugout was not good against such weather. The door shook against its latch and snow came through the wall and settled in the corners. I moved the stove back to the dugout and we retreated there to sit with blankets around our shoulders and watch the glow of the fire in each other's faces.

These were strange quiet moments. We didn't have much to be proud of but I had to allow we were better off than we might have been. I could take satisfaction from the thought that bitter as she was, Molly had never made to leave the place I offered her; and that Jimmy might have done otherwise than jump to work at my side and heed every word I told him. A person cannot live without looking for good signs, you just cannot do it, and I thought these signs were good.

But I looked at Molly sitting near the stove, her head was turned to the side and her hands were folded in her lap and she was gazing at nothing and her eyes were lost listening to the wind and snow outside—and in that quiet moment it was plain to me if she didn't up and leave the first chance she had it was because no other place could she so savor the discouragement of her life. And Jimmy, who worked so willingly, the first day I came to the old town I saw Fee planing a board and his son holding one end for him. I had never once seen the boy linger at something useless the way most children will. He had watched his Pa stumble out of the Silver Sun and he had taken him by the belt—and that was work too. Jimmy was a child fitted to the land, using all his senses to live with what it gave him, and if he did his share and did as I told him why it was because he knew no other way.

Therefore where were my good signs? This green-eyed woman and brown-eyed boy sitting here had never done but the only thing they could do. And I felt like believing we were growing into a true family that was alright: if a good sign is so important you can just as soon make one up and fool yourself that way.

I REMEMBERED THAT HALF BURNT OLD ALMANAC we had and I thought it might be the right weather for teaching the boy to read. I could put a point on a stick and show the letters by scratching them in the floor. So we began to do that, working at it a little each day. I would have him study the letter as it was printed and then say its name and then watch me write it with the stick. Sometimes Molly watched, no expression on her face, maybe she was learning something too.

But the weather was ornery. A storm would blow up for a few days until the snow was banked high enough to keep the inside of the cabin warm. Then the sun would break through for a morning, warm winds would come down from the rocks, and soon everything was melting like a sound of crickets and water running off everywhere. At night the ground iced up, every roof was hung with ice and the cabin walls were exposed again to the cold winds. It went on like that, every snow bringing its chinook to devil the skin, one day you stepped in snow, the next in mud, water soaked in your boots and froze them at night, it was the next worst thing to pure blizzardry, it was weather that wouldn't let you settle.

Molly said one evening: "Here you're going on and on with those damn letters and you don't even see the boy is sick."

Jimmy had coughed once or twice that I'd heard, but I hadn't thought about it. I said: "You're alright aren't you Jimmy?"

"I'm alright."

But the next day he was coughing a lot. Even in the dugout the ground was damp, at night I folded my blanket and put it under him and then sat up listening to him cough and shiver in his sleep. Molly lay on her side on the other side of the stove, I could tell by her back she was wide awake and listening each time the boy coughed.

The next morning Jimmy couldn't get up. He was shuddering under the blanket, his teeth chattered and there was a wheeze to his breath. His face was flushed and his eyes glittery. Molly looked at me like it was my fault he had come up sick.

Straightaway I went to the Russian's. It was a grey

cold morning and there was ice all along the railing and a muddy crust of snow on the ground. Inside his place Zar was pacing up and down and Adah and the three girls were sitting on the meeting chairs and making a breakfast of flour-cakes and sardines. It was cold in there but they all had coats.

"Zar," I said, "I'll trouble you for some whiskey, the boy has caught something on his chest."

"So?" He waved his hand as he paced. "Take, take, there will be no miners again this week, what for do I need whiskey?"

Adah wanted to know what Jimmy's symptoms were like. I told her he had a powerful cough and the chills and fever.

"Well it's the weather for it," the tall girl, Jessie, said, "I'm feeling poorly myself."

"Ain't the weather's your trouble, honey," Mae said to her, "jes the moon."

Adah told me to wait a bit and she went into another room. Zar had built this place not much wider than a railroad car, and there were two rooms at the end of the public room, one in back of the other.

"No customers, only that deadhead Jenks," Zar was saying. He was vexed the way the weather closed off the trail to the mining camp.

"Hey Blue," Mae got up from the table, "that's a mighty fine beard y'workin' up there, you come over of an evenin' and we'll comb it for yuh."

The Chinese had her mouth full and she had to put her hand up while she giggled.

"God's truth," Mae said, "all we ever see now is that Jenks and he ain't good for much more'n polishin' his damn guns. Beard like that'd keep a girl warm these nights."

"And that New Englander Maple," Zar said, "he

does not drink, he does not use the woman, he stays there in my tent. I buy from him I must pay money, a fine way to trade."

Adah came out carrying two bottles. She told me there was turpentine in the little one for rubbing on the boy's legs. In the big bottle was rum, which was better than whiskey, I was to mix it with some hot water and make him swallow as much as he could take. "Nothing like rum for the chest," she told me.

Well I thanked her and went back and did as she said. And for a while it seemed to help. But in the afternoon Jimmy began to shiver again and he wouldn't take any more rum. Each time he coughed his whole body shuddered. Molly fixed up some flour soup with bits of salt beef for supper but he wouldn't eat it.

It began to frighten me hearing that boy cough away like a man, the sound came up from his bowels and pushed his tongue and eyes out and turned his face crimson. We had him wrapped in all the blankets and the fire built up high but he couldn't stop his shivering. I began to feel the awful helpless rage. We fussed with him hour after hour—sitting him up to ease his breathing, laying him down again—but nothing comforted him and he couldn't get to sleep.

It must have been close on midnight and Jimmy began to whimper and look up from one of us to the other. But we didn't know what else to do. There was an unnatural burning in his eyes and his cheeks drew in with each wheezing breath. Molly couldn't look at him any more, she walked back and forth fingering the cross at her throat. When the boy was taken with a heavy fit of coughing she stepped up into the cabin and walked away in the dark.

Then I felt a breeze at my feet and I went into the

cabin after her. She had the door partly open and she was looking across the windy moonlit reach to the Indian's shack. "Mayor," she said, "what will you do if the boy dies, will you bury him beside his Pa?"

She didn't wait for any answer I might have had but went out just in that dress and headed across for John Bear's place, walking that stiff walk of hers, hugging herself against the bite. A great anger rose in me as I closed the door, I could have struck her right then, I was distressed for the boy's illness, I damned her for the grip she had on my life, this unrelenting whore.

A few minutes later the Indian was standing in the dugout looking down at Jimmy. The boy stared back in fear, Bear wore his buffalo robe over his shirt and his black hair hung from under his hat down to his shoulders. They regarded each other and no word was spoken—and then the Indian bent down and tore the top blanket off Jimmy with such suddenness that he cried out and began to cough.

Bear went into his doctoring with a speed that was like solace. He hung the blanket across the doorway leading to the cabin. He put a pot of water on the stove and poked up the fire. When the water was boiling he threw in some herbs he had and in a few minutes the air in the dugout was sweet and steamy. We all watched his moves transfixed: he drew a tin out of his pocket and poured a handful of seed in his palm. Then he kneeled down and looked around the dugout.

"He wants a stone," Molly said to me.

I ran outside and found a flat piece of rock and brought it to him. He began to pound the seed into a powder, when it was well ground it made the sharp odor of mustard. He took some water from our pail and spilled it over the powder till he had a thick paste of earth and mustard. Then, cupping it in one hand he went over to Jimmy and went down on his knees, straddling the boy.

Jimmy began to struggle then, kicking and throwing his arms up, but the Indian just drew back and looked at him until he quietened and turned his face away. Holding the mustard paste in one hand, Bear exposed the boy's chest. Seeing that small white ribbed body made my heart hurt. Bear spread the medicine across from under one arm to the other, up to the throat, down as far as the stomach. Then he pulled down Jimmy's shirt and bound the blanket tight around him.

I will say this, whatever else was to happen John Bear was the best doctor I ever saw, white or red; he had a true talent for healing and it must be owned him.

Before he left he stepped up to Molly and while she stood startled, unwound the thick chain from her throat and dropped the cross at Jimmy's head. He was no Christian but a modest man; Molly had clutched the cross during her healing and he was no one to deny the power of a charm.

THEN CAME THAT LONG DAY AND NIGHT WITH THE wind whipping snow down from the rocks, and inside the dugout, droplets of water prickling the sod walls as the steam rose from the pot on the stove. I kept feeding the fire and filling the pot. Molly sat with the boy propped against her, he was coughing up matter and spitting it into a rag she held to his face. His eyes were smarting from the mustard, his chest ached with the coughing and burned from the poultice, he was in thorough misery. Whenever he made as if to tear the blanket away she held his hands and whispered: "Let it burn, let it burn deep!"

Sometime during that siege Miss Adah came pounding on the door wanting to know how the boy was doing. She wouldn't come in so I had to step outside and we shouted to each other a few moments before she scurried back to the saloon.

Jimmy didn't take anything for supper but during the night, after the snow let up, I thought he was breathing easier. Still he couldn't close his eyes and Molly, laying his head against her breast, put her arms around him. It was an effort for her, she was blushing, she kept looking at me as if she expected me to laugh at her.

There was a panic in her eyes for a moment, she wanted to talk to the boy, to soothe him, but she had trouble with the words. She had to go back a long way to find them:

"I bet you never seen a big city. Molly used to live in New York, did you know that? Oh it's a grand place with stone houses all in rows, and cobbled streets and lamps on each corner that the man comes to light each evening with a long taper. And the carriage buses you see, so shiny and clean, with horses pulling them that are braided in the mane, high stepping. Did you know that...?"

I was sitting with my back to the wall and chewing on a prairie cake and as Molly went on talking I watched her close. The more she talked the easier the words came. The boy's eyes were open and listening and he was breathing heavily, and Molly sat with her own eyes closed as she summoned up her pictures.

"...and each morning I would have a fresh black frock to put on and a white linen apron and a little starched cap to pin to my hair, as clean and starched as a nun I was. And that house! Well you've never seen the likes, a good fifteen rooms, each room fitted out with its own set of furniture and its polished floor of wood and its fancy rug. Why you could disappear into one of those big soft beds. And in the dining room, that was a room just used for eating, can you see that? The table would be covered with a fine cloth tasseled at the edges, and maybe ten settings of pure silver forks and knives and spoons, with three or four glasses at each place for the different waters or wines. And with the people all talking and laughing and the room lit up with candles, in we would come from the kitchen, three or four of us, carrying trays of hot vegetables and buns and a hen, maybe, and a roasted ham to serve to all the ladies and gentlemen. All the ladies and gentlemen . . ."

I will never forget her words. Even after the boy's eyes were closed she sat holding him around, whispering these rememberances. It was the most she ever said about herself, it was the most I ever learned about her. She was speaking the brogue. I had never heard her use it before, and I wouldn't again.

"All the lovely ladies, all the fine gentlemen . . ."

Then her eyes opened and she saw me looking and "Turn away!" she said, her eyes filling with tears. "Don't you dare look at me, turn away!" Even without her telling me I would have had to, such terrible pride was blinding.

Later Molly slipped away from the boy and laid him down in his sleep which was so long in coming. And we each stretched out to get some sleep too. But all the blankets were on Jimmy and after the fire went down it was cold lying there, there was a chill in my bones that made them ache. I couldn't sleep and neither could Molly. I heard her shivering. I moved near her and touched her shoulder and with a cry she rolled over and bundled up to me. "Damn you Mayor," she whispered in my ear, "I swear I can't bear the sight of you!" And I held her as tight as I could, feeling her breast on mine, feeling her breathing, and then the warmth came and I didn't move until she was asleep. I think I had wanted to hold her ever since the fire. My hands were on her back and I could feel the scars under her dress. She was small, so much smaller than she looked. I held her around, pressing her to me and I thought well we're both suffering our lives, only how we do it is different. If it replenishes her to hate me then let her hate me. At the worst her hate is something between herself and herself. And knowing it I was ashamed I had ever felt poorly of her.

SEVEN

Jimmy was slow to get better, his cough lingered for weeks. Molly tended to him each minute of the time and didn't ask any help from me. She cooked him soups, she kept him well wrapped; and on his walking day she held him under the elbows while he slowly stepped around the cabin. On occasion she went to consult with John Bear, bringing the Indian her portion of food. And if she returned with some more treatment Jimmy might have wanted to squawk but he submitted to it without a word. There was something about Molly that commanded him: she went about her ministering shortly, with never a smile, as if in one moment of a too tired patience she would just give him up and leave him to himself.

She had already left me to myself. Our bundling had warmed her only to the point where she hardly acknowledged that I was there in the cabin. She kept busy with the boy and with the steady cold now I was fairly locked in; so that there was not much I could do but take away the slops, or worry would we have fire to last the winter. When Jimmy was on his feet I thought he might want to take up our reading lessons once more. But he didn't seem keen on it, his eyes always wandered to the woman, and what use there was to the almanac; even that I had to myself.

I spent a lot of time studying the almanac. It kept me from brooding or wondering where the Bad Man might be enjoying his winter. It had census figures for the different states and their counties, and the dates they were brought into the Union. I have always been one for that kind of reading. Before I got the fever to go West I was bound out to a lawyer for some months, and it pleasured me to feel the legal cap or read the briefs all salted down with Latin. In all my traveling, whenever I came across a Warrant or a Notice of any kind I never failed to read it through. Some people have a weakness for cards, or whittling, my weakness has always been for documents and deeds and such like.

When I first came to Hard Times it was nothing posted that stopped me, I had a small stake in my money belt and I was riding up to the lodes to earn some more. But there was Fee putting the finishing boards on Avery's two-story saloon, and the sight of him building this place right up off the flat ground struck me somehow. I could think of better places for a carpenter to make his living; not the poorest townsite I'd seen it still didn't look worth his labor, yet Fee was working with an assurance that made me feel ashamed even to question him. In my forty-eighth year, tired out with looking, looking, moving always and wanting I don't know what, I was ready to grant it wasn't the site but the settling of it that mattered. I bought a room off the porch from Hausenfield and I stayed. Later, without much thinking about it, I got a ledger from a traveling notions man; and after I acquired that lawyer's desk and belongings who was going up to work in the lodes, I put the ledger on the desk and in my spare time I began to put down everyone's name and the land they claimed and what properties they owned. I never enjoyed anything more. The town hadn't a promoter, you see, and there were no records for anything. If it ever got big enough to be listed or if the Territory ever needed names for a statehood petition, why I had these documents. A few people like Avery laughed when it went about what I was doing; later, Avery was one of the first to call me Mayor—

But just thinking about it just made the days longer.

ONE COLD AFTERNOON THERE WAS A BANGING on our door and it was Isaac Maple. He came in begging our pardon, he said he'd tried to see Jenks and Zar both, but Jenks was asleep in the stable and Zar was in a mood and wouldn't speak to him.

"See them about what, Isaac?" I said.

He took something from his pocket which I saw to be a small printed calendar. Standing there, with water hanging from his nose, he said: "I mark off the day with this, and s'far as I know it's December the twenty-fifth, Christmas."

Molly and I looked at him. He was waiting for something by way of reply, but all I could think to say was: "Well if that's so Isaac take off your coat and drink some coffee with us." At the same time Molly looked from him to me and walked away without a word.

It was clear in his eyes we were as bad as Jenks or the Russian. His sad hound's face fell: "Thank ye, no," he said and turned and went out.

That put him in my mind for the rest of the day. Isaac Maple stayed alone in his tent most of the time, thinking I suppose of his brother Ezra. He was a shy man and he was new to the West and it must have been a powerful need for comfort which brought him to our door. I don't often honor holidays but I wanted to understand Isaac's feelings. In the evening I went over to Zar's place and demanded a drink on the house.

Zar was leaning with his elbows on his sawhorse bar: "For what," he scowled at me.

"It's Christmas, Zar," I said. "Didn't you know?"

"Wal wal, I tell you—only the spring shall I celebrate."

But Miss Adah was properly moved. She ran to wake up the girls sleeping in the back rooms. I thought she had just the spirit Isaac wanted and when she came back I said, "Isaac Maple's the one who told me."

"I'll go get him," she said putting a shawl over her. "Poor man's all alone."

"Save yourself, Adah," Zar said, but she was gone.

Zar had no use for the man and couldn't see going to any trouble over him; when Adah returned, leading Isaac Maple, she had to set up the drinks herself the Russian had sat down, grumbling, on one of his camp chairs.

Then Jenks wandered in, he was wearing a hat he'd made out of prairie dog fur, it came down to his eyes and went around his head to a point in back. You could just about make out his wolfy smile under that cap.

"The customer," Zar said folding his arms.

Well I saw it was going to be a true enough gathering so I took myself back to the cabin to get Molly and the boy. Molly wanted no part of it. She said it wouldn't do for Jimmy to go out at night with the wind so cold and snow blowing along the ground. I said we could wrap a blanket around him and I'd carry him over. That didn't please either of them too much, but then we heard, coming across the wind, the sounds of Miss Adah's voice singing a hymn with her melodeon, and I did as I wanted—wrapping the boy up—and we all went over.

When we came in Adah stopped her singing and got up to greet Molly. Everyone was very polite—Jenks pulled at his cap when he said hello and the ladies gave Jimmy a greeting although, since he stood by Molly's side, they stayed their distance. There was only one lantern on the table and the room was in shadows, but Zar got up to light another and at Adah's signal he started to pour out a drink for Molly. She held up her hand, very ladylike, and smiled and shook her head. She had drunk her share in the old days and it wouldn't have hurt her now, but it gave her more pleasure to refuse, it set her apart from the ladies although she knew them better than they thought she did.

All at once, as we were standing around, nobody had anything to say, we were all embarrassed we'd made an occasion. I lifted my cup: "Well here's to Christmas and better times for the world."

"Amen," said Miss Adah. Then she sat down at the melodeon and began her hymn again. Everyone was quiet and drinking listening to her sing it through. She had a deep voice but she meant what she sang. When she finished she started another and it was one Isaac recognized, he stepped up in back of her and looking straight at the wall he joined right in, tenor.

Well the whiskey was warm going down and it spread over me like sun. There was the churchly music going; Molly, with Jimmy at her side, was sitting on a chair listening; Zar was stepping around offering the bottle; and I thought why this is what Isaac Maple had in mind, just to celebrate the fact that all of us are here. And I asked myself whether these weren't already better times: here was some people and we had a root on the land where there was nothing but graves a few months before.

After a while the liquor began to have its effect on everyone. Jessie and Mae, who had been cowed by Molly's presence, made a show of forgetting she was there and began to enjoy themselves. Jessie went over to Jenks, sitting in a chair, and stuck her thumb under his fur cap.

"Is that you under there, Dead-Eye?" she said.

Jenks slapped her hand away, stealing a glance at Molly at the same time: "Get on!"

"Why Jenksy!" said Mae plunking herself down on his lap. "Ah've never seen you so outdone. Didn't you get yore sleep t'day?"

"If'n hew please, ladies," Jenks said pushing Mae off. Holding his drink high he walked away to the bar. Jessie and Mae giggled. Jenks was being uncommon dignified but pieces of drying dung were stuck to the seat of his pants.

When the hymn was ended Adah turned in her seat and put her hand on Isaac's arm: "You sing right nice, Mr. Maple," she said.

"Thank ye, I like a good hymn," said Isaac.

Zar was clapping his hands: "Holy, holy, holy! That's vary good."

"Ye have a true gift Miss Adah," Isaac said.

"A gift?" said Zar. "Together you and she—two coyotes howling at moon."

Isaac turned to him: "Say what?"

"Sure!" Zar began to laugh. "Such music I have heard on the steppe at night. Just the same as that: Howly, howly, howly!" He doubled up with his own joke. "Jassie, Mae, you hear?" And he repeated what he'd said.

But the girls were busy working on Jenks, they had followed him to the bar.

"What's botherin' your friend tonight, Mae," said Jessie.

"He's jes shy," Mae said digging Jenks in the ribs.

"I smelled o' horseshit I'd be shy too," Jessie said.

"I'll tell you frand," Zar walked up to Isaac. "Not only your singing is not human, but your way of doing business. A man would trade for my liquor. A man would have need for my girls."

"Ain't nobody can tell me how to run my business," Isaac said turning red in the face.

"Cash cash!" Zar threw his head back: "Caaash!"

"Nobody forcing ye to buy!" Isaac shouted over the Russian's roar.

Adah thought things were getting out of hand, she glanced once at Molly and turned around to play another hymn. But it only added to the noise. Zar walked away from Isaac with a gesture of disgust and poured himself another drink from the bottle on the table. The storekeep was following him, well aroused.

"Did I not pay ye cash for the use of yer tent? I deal fair and square, always have, always will. All's I look fer is an honest profit and that's more'n some can say!"

"Who needs you," said Zar.

"God knows I didn't ask to stay here, I was asked!"

By this time the smiles were gone from Mae's and Jessie's faces.

"I b'lieve Mr. Jenks here has gone fancy on us Mae."

"Listen you no-chinned, gun polishing deadhead," said Mae, "the next time you come along with yo' tongue hangin' out don't look for us. Jes keep agoin' down to *her* place and see what *she'll* give you."

"You bucktooth son of a bitch," said Jessie pushing

her face up to Jenks. For a second I thought Molly had heard, but the melodeon was blowing loud and Isaac Maple was shouting over it.

"I was horse-traded! Yessir," he looked right at me, "I'll say it. Horse-traded! Paid out good money to settle in this Hell. 'Tweren't fit country fer Ezra and 'tain't fit fer me!"

"Didn't it never snow in Vermont, Isaac?"

"It did, yes it did. But you could reckon it, you didn't spend yer days and nights beatin' the sag out of a tent to keep from bein' buried!"

"Why this is a gentle winter, Isaac," I said.

"That may be but it's m' first and last in this hole, I'll tell ye."

"Than go and farewell," Zar screamed.

"I'll go, I will, don't ye fret. When that stage comes I'll be on it when it goes—"

At that moment Miss Adah stopped her song. And in the sudden silence Isaac looked around and cried: "But that stage'll never come. We'll all be dead before that stage comes again!"

Those were the lonesomest words I nearly ever heard. Not a night had passed lately when I hadn't thought the same thing; but I'd never said it out loud and neither had anyone else. Isaac took the fear in all our minds and put it in the air. A chill ran through the room and in the quiet we heard the wind outside blowing desolate across the earth. I saw a wilderness of snow-crusted flats between us and the rest of the world, and not a track on it.

A moment later Isaac left. Then Molly got up and went off quickly. Mae leaned against the bar and fingering her hair said: "See you next Christmas, honey," softly, as to herself. Zar slumped down at a table and put his head on his hand. Our gathering didn't make any more sense, each of us was alone as himself, I wrapped up the boy and we left too.

THE FORLORN FEELING OF THAT CHRISTMAS NIGHT grew as time went on. There were days of such pure cold that it was like swallowing frost to take a breath out of doors. The weather had us holed up good, almost in spite it seemed like, and if I thought about the spring it was as a lost possibility. How could you remember the warmth of the sun when through one bleak day after another the winter danced around you with every fancy step it knew? We huddled in that cabin, bent grey sticks with eyes in them, I couldn't even worry that one day we might not have what to eat or make a fire with: it was a worse dread to feel so lost on the earth, a live creature in a lifeless land.

What I'm trying to do now is account for the way things went, this winter had a lot to do with it. Under such conditions even the plain doings of a day had no reason. It was foolishness to eat just to stay alive inside that room; it was foolishness to lie down for the night since you would only wake up to the same day again. Once Molly looked at the door and said: "We're buried as sure as those people frozen in the ground out there! Oh Christ but we know it, that's all difference." And Jimmy, with that picture of his father, jumped up hugging her and crying as if to make it not true.

Sometimes we could hear through the wind the awful rows Zar made with his ladies. It sounded like murder. The Russian was drinking up his own stock and it made him mean. He knocked a tooth out of the tall girl Jessie's mouth and on one occasion Miss Adah had to put him to sleep with a stick, he was going at the Chinagirl so.

Leo Jenks took to walking out in the storms and firing his guns into the wind. Once he stayed out too long, claiming he had seen a pronghorn; he may have or he may not, but his fingers froze to his rifle and when he stumbled into Zar's place they pried it loose and the skin went with it.

And Isaac Maple kept to himself in that tent, marking off each day as a mistake on his pocket calendar. He never talked when you went to buy something from him, not trusting in any exchange of words, but got you out again as quick as he could. On an especially bitter day, when the wind made your teeth ache and froze your lashes, he went around to each of us in turn —Zar, Jenks, me, and then over to the Indian—offering to sell a partner's half of what he had on order with Alf Moffet. Nobody would buy and this convinced him that he was right, that he'd been horse-traded and that Alf would not show up again. From then on he charged us double his price for flour and sardines— which is all he had left—and finally he refused to sell altogether, claiming he needed the food for himself.

When this happened Zar came to see me with his shotgun, saying: "Let's kill him." Zar meant what he said, but I did some talking and instead we trudged over to the stable, where Jenks was nursing his sore hands, and we took a look at the horses. They all had loose hides and hanging heads. What feed there was they had eaten up, where there was bark on the stalls they had chewed it off. The Major's pony seemed worse than the rest, his eyes were dull, his bones stuck out and he had ulcers all over his legs. I borrowed Jenk's pistol and shot the pony behind the ear.

Not one of the other animals stirred with the sound.

Zar took the gun and killed one of his team; and we spent the afternoon dressing down the carcasses. It was something we would have had to do sooner or later, what Isaac did was just as well, another week and there wouldn't have been any meat to dress down. I got back to the cabin, my hands and feet were numb and my clothes were stiff with blood, but there was a cache in the snow outside the door that would keep us awhile.

We used everything of that poor thin pony, a splinter from his ribs made a needle and his sinew made thread. There was no bark to tan with, but Molly fleshed the hide with the stiletto and for days she beat it with a stone, rubbed it with dirt. She finally got it soft, although she didn't think she would, and she sewed up a rough jacket for the boy. And I made us covers for our shoes. I will say here that all this—even the slaughtering—helped my spirits. It was doing something purposeful. Molly too worked with a will. But I suppose Jimmy had an attachment for that pony, and although he wore the jacket when it was done, and ate the soup Molly cooked from the bones, he didn't bother to look at me any more.

Of all the miseries of that winter not the least was waking up to Jimmy's dislike. I don't believe in the human intelligence of animals, or that they are to be used in any way but the most useful; I didn't think when I shot that pony but that it was something that had to be done. However the boy made me regret it. You see once I saw how he felt it made me realize that his feeling was nothing sudden, but like a divide that had risen between us as time went on. I felt less close to him now than the night I sat up with him when his Daddy died. How many ponies had I killed besides this one?

Molly had no such trouble with the boy's affections, many times she would say something to him that I thought cruel, or she would look at him like he was nothing but the orphan boy he was—but her treatment only made him doggish. Since his illness he had gotten this way, following her with his eyes and waiting patiently for whatever morsel of attention she might throw him. Now I could see in Molly's face a shadow like she didn't want him so. It unsettled her, it was nothing she asked for. If I regretted some of the love he gave her I'm sure she did too. I can't be too clear about that, it makes me sad to remember. It wasn't until a night about two weeks after the horse killings that I felt properly frozen for the winter.

In the dugout something brought us all awake. It was an unearthly scratching sound. I turned up the lamp and we followed it with our eyes. There was an animal on the roof, scratching at the warmth. I grabbed my gun and just as I did a slat was pushed away, and in a fine sift of snow a thick tawny paw slipped in from the night and clawed at the air above Molly's head. She screamed. I shot once, twice, not at the paw but through the wood where the heart would be. The paw was gone before my second shot. I thought of the meat we had left outside the door and ran to it, holding the lamp, and from the open door I saw in the dim cast of lamplight a shadow bounding off through the snow. Well the crash was still in my ears and my heart was banging hard when I went around to put the board back in place; and I can't forget the sight, looking down through there, Molly and Jimmy were hugging each other for all their lives, they were fastened in their terror. After that she got to be as doggish to him as he was to her. She was no longer put out by his regard, but took care of him warmly, often giving him kisses. And I don't think any of us but me kept remembering, always with a banging heart, the sight of those claws, sharp as scythes, swiping at us from the night.

THERE HAD TO BE AN END TO WINTER OR AN END to us. By the time March came in I was ready, like Isaac Maple, to bet with the winter. Hard dry winds blew day after day, sweeping the snow, skimming the top of the bared frozen ground and blowing up circly storms of sand. But one afternoon I thought I smelled rain. I went outside: John Bear was standing over by his shack, he was facing west and looking into the dusty bleak sky—he had smelled it too. The air was cold but the wind was just a murmur of what it had been, and if you stood very still you could feel now and then a warmth in it, a dampness. I kept my hopes to myself but that night I woke up and heard it, a soft fall on the roof, not a shower but a small steady rain. And at dawn the sun spread over the flats with a rush.

I stepped outside into that new morning and I couldn't believe it. The sun filled my eyes with a warmth of hazes, pink, pale green and yellow, and all over the flats white mists were rising like winter being steamed out of the ground. I swore I could feel the earth turning. Everything was new in my sight, I looked around at the short street of buildings—cabin, windmill, saloon, tent and stable—and it seemed like a row of plants just sprung. The Chinese girl peeked out of the saloon, holding her hand up against the brilliance, and I waved to her. A few minutes later everyone was out of doors, blinking in the sunlight, standing silent in the face of something that was hard to remember. Then Jenks gave a hoot and threw his hat into the air and all of a sudden everyone was stretching, calling out, Zar went around hugging everybody, Adah was shaking Isaac Maple's hand, the girls were kissing each other, Jimmy was holding Molly's arm and pulling her this way and that. Jenks went into his stable and drove the horses out, there was much mingling, we were all smiling like fools, we were all pasty and thin in the fresh light but alive even so.

EIGHT

Now I WOULD WRITE ABOUT THAT SPRING IN ITS
every minute if I could, using up my strength and time
and going no further through the pain of seasons. But
it is no pleasure to me now; and it is all I can do to
remember it for my purposes which is to tell the way
things happened.

This was the time when Swede settled and Bert Albany came down, the hurts were healing in the warm
sun and the expectations were nourished into life. A
greenness of hopes grew up like the scrub along the
rocks coming up green.

I remember another spring, much before, when I
repped with an outfit that ranged along the Big Mo:
how the river thawed with great groans and cracks,
and the ice broke and rose in the air to be carried off
in the surge, until the water had its full bed and was
running swiftly from one bank to the other. It was a
grand rout of winter. Well the change was just as sudden here, a bit of sun drew all the frost from our bones
and the blood ran swift in our veins. Alf Moffet pulled
in with his coach low on its springs for all the freight it
carried, and the miners began to ride down again.
They had been working most of the winter and they all
had a hankering to spend some of their pay somewhere
besides the company stores. In a couple of Saturday

nights Isaac Maple forgot he'd been horse-traded, he and Zar, too, made enough to start bringing Alf back regular every two weeks. With my commission on their orders I made enough to buy up a stock of tinned food, coffee, sugar, flour, saleratus, beans and salt pork. And I'll tell you we commenced to eat good.

Each morning and night Molly would do up a batch of pancakes and we dipped them in sugar and ate them rolled. We had beans and pork and maybe whole tomatoes from a can, and good black coffee to wash it all down. We ate till we couldn't remember the taste of that horse, and it wasn't long before the flesh filled in between the bones and we began to look human once more.

We were still ragged as Indians but with the sun rising higher each day the need for Hausenfield's well rose too; and I fixed a price of a dollar a day for every person who drew from it. I was lucky with the windmill, I nailed the blades back up and fixed some loose boards in the scaffold and it worked fine, bringing the water up fresh and cool, bringing up the dollars. I went into Isaac's tent one day and I walked out with a miner's jacket and small-sized boots for Jimmy, laced shoes and calico for Molly, and a razor for myself.

I remember that alright. Straightaway I went over to the well, put those things down and found a rock to hone my new razor, and with the piece of lye soap there I shaved off my beard right down to the skin. I had not shaved since I lost my old razor in the fire, and it was something I had been itching to do ever since. Although like most I favor mustaches, I am not given to beards, I don't like their feel nor the way the lice will take to them. When I was done—feeling slick as a calf—I took those things into the cabin and you should have seen the looks on their faces. Molly and the boy went into a proper reverence, I don't know whether it was the new things or me. "Well look at that," said Molly, smiling, and I think she meant me.

Jimmy was all smiles too—until Molly made up her mind he would have to wash himself before he could put the jacket and boots on. So he had to go outside and sit in the tub and while he did Molly took his pants and shirt and scrubbed them down in a pail of water. Later Miss Adah, always of a generous turn of mind, came out of the saloon and offered Molly a scissors. What surprised me was Molly took it, what surprised Jimmy was that she put it to his head. When he was all done, dressed in new boots and a jacket, and a clean dry shirt and pants, with some of his hair trimmed— well he was angry but he looked fine. "A proper boy," Molly said, gazing at him.

Molly was fair to look on as she said that. Just the day before she had washed her hair and gone to sit up in the rocks aways to let the breeze dry it. She had handsome features for all the pockings, the frown was gone from her forehead and there was a softness in her face, a measure of joy in her eyes. I couldn't grudge her hold on Jimmy, they were doing each other good, maybe giving each other a rest from the past, why should I have felt anything but glad?

All I am describing happened on an afternoon of deep gold sunlight over everything, with air that was sweet to breathe. Over by his shack John Bear was fooling with his garden. Jessie was working one too, she didn't know and I wasn't going to tell her that only the Indian could raise anything out of this ground. Smoke was coming up from Zar's still behind his saloon. Away in the distance Zar and Jenks were running out their horses in big circles over the flats. There was a feeling of celebration in everything that was going on.

I WENT OVER TO JENKS'S STABLE AND LOOKED OVER his horses one morning, it was not the boy's feelings I had in mind, you just don't like to be without something to ride. I liked the looks of the mule best of all, his ribs showed through his hide but he'd wintered better than the grey or the sorrel. Knowing my man I went to Jenks and told him I wanted to buy one of his horses. A sly look came into his eyes and he told me he'd deal only for the mule. We settled on the sum of seventy-five dollars, to be paid in water rights at a dollar a day not including days of rain, if any. I took out the mule and brought him around to the cabin and hitched him to the buckboard. He stood there the best part of a day until Jimmy wandered over like he didn't care, and hefted the reins like it didn't mean anything and finally stepped up on the seat and give him a try in the flats.

It gladdened me to see him romp off that way. Pretty soon he came back in but it was just to pull Molly, protesting, up on the seat; and then there they were spinning away, she laughing and holding on tight and Jimmy shouting in a cracked voice, standing up and flipping those reins and getting more and more run out of the mule. I went about my business and it seems now just a moment before I turned around and they were hardly in view. They had made circles further and further out but all I saw was a funnel of dust going down in a straight line. Where were they going? For a moment my breath stopped, I thought well good-bye to them, it serves me right, they're gone and she's still laughing.

But Jimmy had only seen something and gone to take a closer look. For a long time the rig was a black spot in my eye and finally it moved; and a while after they were back at the cabin.

"What's out there Jimmy?" I said.

He looked at Molly. She got down and went inside and he followed her.

I went after. "I said what's out there, boy, where's your voice?"

"Wagon." Another look at Molly. Her mouth was set tight.

"One wagon?"

"Yes." And then with a rush: "It's busted in the back and the man's settin' up there and she's screamin' at him."

"Who is?"

"Why that woman, she's—"

"Jimmy!" Molly said.

"Who are they?" I turned to her.

"How should I know who?"

"Well didn't you speak to them?"

"Oh sure! I'll go around greetin' every lowlife on the prairie!"

I went out and found Zar and told him what they'd seen. He was busy with his still but he said I could take his team and wagon. I hitched up four and Jenks reckoned he'd come along and we got up and started off. Why was I taking Zar's wagon and not the mule and rig? I guess Molly understood better than I: we passed the cabin and she came out of the door, Jenks tipped his hat to her but she cried: "I know what you're doing! Go get 'em Mayor, more fools for your town!"

We found it due south, sitting on the trail that edged

the flats: it was just as Jimmy said, an old Murphy wagon stuffed to its cover, a man was sitting on the box and the back wheels of the wagon were splayed out like a new colt's legs. The man was yellow-haired and beardless, his hands hung down between his knees and he watched us with eyes as baleful as his oxen's. No woman was screaming at him, but further off walking away through the scrub with a shawl over her head she was raising her arms and shouting at the sky.

The man said: "Ay ben looking for Svedes."

I said: "Well there's none hereabouts so far as I know."

He nodded as if he didn't expect otherwise. Jenks and I climbed down to take a look at the axle, and when we did the man stepped off his box and he was the tallest fellow I ever saw, he must have been six and a half feet. He walked clumsy like a big man; he was fair-complected with strawberry skin, on the side of his neck there was a wen the size of a cannonball.

The axletree was split clean through, each half was poking into the ground. "You carrying another one?" I said.

"No. No oder."

Off aways the woman kept shouting, it was the only sound in our ears and the man got embarrassed. "My vife," he said tapping his forehead and he smiled ruefully.

"You a nester?" Jenks said looking up at him.

"Ya, I vas."

Jenks nodded: "Prairie'll do hit—"

"Ya." We all looked at the axle. "She beg me for tree yar go wit oder Svedes. Cry each night. . . . But I hope rain vill come. But no rain. Now I look for Svedes, maybe her mind comes back."

Swede's voice was as deep as the lowing of a cow, but it was a gentle voice with no harshness to it. He didn't cry about his misfortune but told it straight. I liked him right off. I told him there wasn't much we could do about the axle but he could put up in the town awhile and maybe get hold of another by and by. He agreed to that so we started to unload his gear. We spent a good hour putting it on Zar's wagon, these people were carting everything they'd ever owned. There was a frame bed, a bureau with four drawers, an oak table, a commode, bedding, chairs, stools, a churn, a kettle, a washtub, some iron pots, a plow with a steel share, a sack of corn—it was no wonder their old wagon gave out.

The woman had come back to peek at us while we worked and it unsettled Jenks to catch her staring around the side of the wagon. It didn't bother me none. She was a stocky woman, when her shawl slipped it showed her hair which was light-colored and sparse, her face was honest enough but there was nothing to hold on to in her eyes.

I'd worked up a good thirst by the time we were through. There was about another hour of sun left in the sky. I said: "Your wagon should pull now with nothing on it. We'll tote your things in, you follow us straight that way."

"Good. Helga!" he called to the woman. He went over to her and began to talk to her as to a child, pointing to Jenks and me. Without any warning she started screaming at him and then hitting him. She barely came high as his chest but she swung up and slapped his face again and again and beat at his arms. He made no move to stop her but just stood waiting for her to spend herself.

111

"Godamighty," Jenks said.

"Let's get up on the wagon," I said. It put our backs to the sight, I didn't like to see something like that.

"Godamighty," Jenks swore as we sat waiting, "a jahnt lahk thet a sufferin' sich blows!"

After a while we didn't hear anything and as I turned the man was lifting his wife to the back of our wagon, sitting her on a chair so that she faced rearwards. She made no protest and he said: "You vill see me, Helga, ya?" We started off, the horses pulling hard, and I didn't have to hold them, the weight did that. Behind us the man snapped his quirt over the oxen and they began to draw the covered wagon. It wobbled but it went, the axle scratching a furrow in the ground.

When we were back at the town the man was still halfway across the flats. "Leave everything be until he gets here," I told Jenks. He went into Zar's place and in a moment Zar and his ladies came out to look, and Isaac Maple from his tent. Molly and Jimmy came over, everyone stared up at the woman on the wagon. The ladies went around to the side to look at all the furniture. Not one word was spoken and the woman sat still up on the chair keeping her gaze out to the flats where her husband was coming. I went to the well for a drink and when I looked back I saw the woman bend over with her hands on her knees, and she spat at Molly's feet.

Well in a moment Molly was by me at the well. I thought it was anger giving her tremors but she was grey with fear. "Now Molly," I said, and she allowed me to hold her arm, "that's nothing but a poor old nester's wife."

And that was how Bergenstrohm came to settle. But we never called him anything but Swede.

IT WAS ISAAC MAPLE WHO TOOK THE COUPLE UNder care. Everyone else was put off by the woman's madness but Isaac said: "My mother had spells from her change of life, my grandmother 'fore her, I seen it since I was a boy it don't bother me." He offered his tent for storing their furniture. He had Swede pull his wagon alongside of the tent and the two of them propped up the back with rocks. They put the bed and bureau back in the wagon and Isaac said, "Ye kin keep a nice house in there fer the time bein'."

He must have decided right off to give them credit. He paid me a dollar a day for their water although I told him there was no need. He thumbed through one of his catalogues and found a steel axle he could order that would fit the old Murphy wagon. He was taking care of the Swede like he was his own brother.

"Wal," Zar said to me one day, "is no meestery. The man has wagon." That was true as far as it went, Isaac needed something to fetch lumber in if he wanted to build himself a proper store; until now Zar's wagon was the only one he might have had, and he would sooner have given up his plans than ask for it. But I have a feeling Isaac would have welcomed these people had they only a handcart. I think it was enough that they had come to the town after him. Isaac was the kind of chary person who's always looking for someone to trust. He couldn't trust any of us who'd been there before him; but the Swede came off the flats as he himself had the autumn before, and that was as good as a ticket from Vermont.

Whatever his feelings Isaac didn't stand to lose much. You figure anyone who keeps a mad wife will pay his debts and do his share of work. Long before Alf delivered the axle it was clear that the man was worthy, gentle for all his size, he would ask no favors and do any asked of him. His woman seemed calmer with people around; and after one Saturday he didn't again speak of looking for Swedes. What happened was one of the miners found Helga with her washtub and gave her fifty cents to wash his corduroys. The diggers were feeling the spring and they had a great wish to spiff up. It got to be a usual sight, a bunch of men standing around in back of Swede's wagon in only their high lacers and union suits, smoking Isaac Maple's imported Regalias or Cheroots and talking like members of a Society. Swede enjoyed their business and their talk. He would build a fire and hang a line of rope over it to dry the things his wife washed, and he'd stand trading words with the men, telling his story nodding his big head as he listened to theirs. . . .

I can't deny how I felt seeing this farmer settle in the town. Molly was right, I would welcome an outlaw if he rode in. I felt anyone new helped bury the past. Swede's coming even put in my mind a thought I wouldn't have tolerated before—to keep a record again, to write things down. Alf had left me three ledgers and a steel-point pen to keep the Express accounts. But there was enough paper in the ledgers to write the Bible. It was an idea that I had to put away, I looked toward Molly as if I expected her to read my thoughts, and I almost set myself against the words of scorn that would come.

Actually, once Swede and his wife were here to stay

Molly didn't say a word against them. Something about Helga had scared her into gentleness, and it was like you find a drunkard who's sworn off, having been cowed by the vision of Hell. Molly was never inclined to welcome a new face but for a long while she would not say so, her judgment was softened. When Bert Albany came down and I found out why, I told Molly and she even smiled.

BERT CAME WALKING DOWN THE TRAIL IN THE middle of one week, his shoulders were hunched and he sighed like he was carrying the world with him. He was the same pimply boy who always posted his letters with me. He stood in front of Zar's place, smoothing the ground with his boot and finally he made up his mind to go in. "Don't you know this is working day?" Zar said to him.

The young fellow didn't answer and he looked ashamed. He sat around in the saloon all day, sighing and nursing whiskeys, and he didn't speak to anyone. Zar struggled to understand what the boy's trouble was and he finally decided Bert had lost his job. "Poor boysik, he will not say bot I know he must have lost favor with the mine boss."

Now how was that so? Bert was not more than twenty. As well as I could remember he always got drunk when he came to town—not because he seemed to enjoy it but because it put him in company with the rest of the diggers. That's the way a young fellow does, doing twice as much of anything to make sure he keeps up with the rest. The mine boss wouldn't let go someone like Bert. But Zar said, "Ah, I can afford him a

few dollars, I will take him on as helper," so I kept my
views to myself.

When the Russian offered him the job Bert's mouth
dropped open. Then his face lit up and he laughed.
Course he'd take it! A couple of days after this I spoke
to him: "Well," I said, "now you don't have to travel
but a few steps to post your letters."

"Hell, Mr. Blue," he said, "I given up writin' letters. Never got no letters back." He was cheerful saying this, he didn't seem to mind. And each morning
there was a new sound to hear, Bert whistling as he
went about his chores.

On a Thursday evening I stepped into Zar's place
for a drink. Jenks was there, sitting at a table with Mae
and Jessie. I could hear where Zar was—his snores
were coming out of the side room like running cattle.
Miss Adah served me from behind the bar. "Where's
the new man?" I said to her.

She looked over at the two girls and they looked
back. Mae got up and went to the door to the side
room and closed it carefully.

"Now listen Blue, please," Adah said to me in a low
tone, "you got to promise to keep this under your
hat."

Jessie and Mae came up on either side of me and I
found myself hard put to raise the cup.

"What's going on ladies?"

"That Bert is sparkin' our little girl," Adah said.

"Whut's thet?" Jenks had followed. "The Chink?"

"Jenks I sweah," Mae turned on him with a harsh
whisper, "an you say one word I'll have yo' scalp!"

"Gwan back to your stable, deadhead," said Jessie,
"this don't concern you."

Jenks leaned back with his elbows on the bar and he

grinned that sly grin of his: "Shit . . . Y'mean he's cooin' wif thet li'l yaller flopgal?"

"Hush damn you," Adah said. She looked at me: "It's no joke, Zar finds out and he'll kill him."

"He's really struck on her?" I said.

"Lord!" said Jessie. "You've never seen the like. You'd think she was white. You'd think she had a papa owned a railroad!"

"Saturday he didn't give nobody else a chance to touch her," Adah said. "Paid her the money and took her out by the well and held her hand."

"I saw it," Mae said nodding.

"Godamighty!" Jenks said.

"Then after a while she figures it's time to come back in, and so in he follows and gives her the money again and out they go again."

"Well what do you know!" I had to laugh. "Zar thought he was fired from his job."

"No sir, he just up an' quit it! That boy's crazy, he's wild! There's no tellin' what he'll do why I never saw a person afflicted so."

Jenks said: "Knew a feller oncet were bedded to a Piute. She sure did have a scent."

"It don't seem right," Mae said biting on her finger-nail.

"I don't know," I said.

"Now Blue," said Adah, "that little thing is besides herself. She was so scairt Saturday she couldn't keep from shakin' all over."

"It scares her?"

"Why she's been cryin' ever since. He has her out there somewhere right now moonin' like a sick calf over her, poor thing she don't know what to do."

"Well if he's taken a fancy for her," I said, "there are worse things."

"Blue," said Adah, "there are fancies and fancies. She's just a child, she don't understand that kind of business, he got no sense treating her like that."

"When Zar finds out he'll kill 'em both," Mae said.

"Well Zar don't own the girl. Any of you could take a beau if you really wanted," I said.

"Maybe we could, maybe we couldn't," Jessie said. "But he bought her. Paid her Pa a hundred dollars."

"That Chink weren't even her Pa," Mae said to Jessie. "He said he was but he didn't look as he could sire a flea."

"You won't let on will you Blue?"

"I'm dumb ladies."

"Poor child," said Adah, "there's no telling what'll happen. What is it possesses that boy I don't hope to guess."

I downed the drink and there were these three glum faces around me—weary Miss Adah with her fine mustache, long-jawed Jessie, Plump Mae, her cheeks going to fat . . . What Zar would do worried them, but I think they were more frightened by Bert himself. They were uneasy at such a feeling in someone, it was beyond them. For me it was a revelation that such a thing was happening here. It was like someone had come along to put up a flag. I made up my mind if Zar raised a ruckus like the ladies feared I would do what I could for the boy. I wanted to nurture something like that, keep it going.

The more I thought about Bert the better I liked him. You like to see desperation still in its pimples. I went to Isaac's tent and the Swede was there, and I told them about Bert. They had a good laugh. When I went back to the cabin Molly was sitting outside. We'd been having some afternoons of sweet rain, some evenings of slow-dying skies, and she'd taken to sitting on a stool in front of the cabin door and she'd watch the night come on. I sat down near her and I could just feel the smile when I told her there was a true lover come to town.

Then there was silence between us and I see no reason now not to put down what happened: I found myself aware of Molly in a way that was pleasure and pain at the same time. I felt her closeness. I kept thinking I was older than she was and you see it was a too familiar thought to have, I had no right to it. I was not Bert Albany, I wasn't free to respect my feelings, and so nothing was said as the darkness came down. And when she went inside I sat still and waited until she would be asleep before I followed.

But that following Saturday was the night it first appeared all our fortunes were changing. There was a big crowd of miners and they were feeling the season, their carryings-on was not just a bit of fun, it was liken to a shivaree. They brought mouth organs with them, one fellow came up with a banjo, there was a lot of dancing with the drinking and since the women were scarce among so many, the miners danced with each other, stomping out squares so as to make the ground shake. And insisting in all that noise was talk of a new stamping mill going up not far to the east. The China-girl had no worries about Zar that night. Bert kept her in sight of his bar all the time but the Russian wouldn't have noticed if he had carried her around on his shoulders: Zar was blinded happy with the rumors, rushing around from one fellow to the next to hear every version. By midnight he'd decided the company was going to lay a road down the trail from the mines so as to cart the ore to the new mill—

I didn't trust myself to believe him. But it is true that the town was to be blessed with luck; and some of it was even to rub off on me.

NINE

I THOUGHT IF ZAR'S MIND WAS A PONY IT WOULD win the race. I wanted nothing to do with his happy expectations. But every time something else came up to justify them he would laugh at me, saying: "Wal, frand, am I crazy?" Until I had to go with the signs and tell him one day: "No, by God, Zar, you're saner than me."

Now you have to season the talk of a digger with a lot of salt. A digger's a man who'll look for pay dirt twenty years of days with just as much fervor and high hope the last day as the first. Why any time you're near one you can hear his song: "I'm savin' my money Jack, and as soon as I have me a grubstake, it's good-bye to the Company. I'm off to Montany and find me that vugg of pure gold! I know where it is, I know the spot Jack, it's jest a sittin' and a waitin' fer me...." And he buys Jack a drink on it; and they both believe it. I didn't want to put stock in any rumor come down from the camp.

But there was a stamping mill gone up, that was a fact. Alf told me it too: a town called Number Six and it was maybe fifteen miles dead east. Angus Mcell-henny told me something else: The Company shipped on the toll roads leading west from the camp, so it didn't pay them to cart anything but high-grade ore.

But if they cut a road down to us they could get to the new mill across the flats and pay no toll to anyone. And they could make their low grade pay off as well.

The way Angus spoke the idea made sense. And then one morning, early, a man rode down from the lodes and he had a string of mules trailing him. I'd never seen him before but I knew who he was, I'd heard him cursed too many times not to know him, Archie D. Brogan, the mine boss. He had pale-blue eyes in a face of fat, he was much too beefy for the miner's garb he wore. He sat around drinking and jittery until Alf Moffet drove in with the stage, and then we knew why Brogan had come: Three men in black tailored suits and derby hats stepped out and he nearly fell all over himself giving them a proper welcome. They were small men and they stepped precisely in our dirt, but they were the directors from the East and their engineer; so we cheered as Brogan put them on the mules and took them, bouncing, up the trail to the lodes.

"I shall build a hotel!" Zar cried after them and he even hugged Isaac Maple in his joy.

A few days later the Company men came back down to meet a special coach. And while waiting they fanned themselves with their derbies. "I never seen men with such white hands," Adah said in a whisper, "why it's indecent!" They talked to nobody, only asking Zar, at one point, if he carried wine. Zar was anguished because he didn't, and when they rode off he shook his fist after them: "I shall build a hotel!" It was a vow this time and somehow it made the prospect surer.

Not long afterwards we had a visit from a man owned a public house along the toll road leading west from the camp, and he looked us over carefully and measured out a lot for himself next to Swede's wagon; and without my saying a word he put a ten-dollar gold piece in my hand—to hold it—and he rode away saying he'd be back.

Well you see all this was a bloom in the heart, a springing of hope, and even when I tried to tell myself it was just like the afternoon sun—so cozying on the face, like a warm hand, that a man could dream of anything and expect it—even when I pressed myself with doubts, the hope squeezed out like a nectar. And as I sat with Molly another evening under the sky, with a new moon making us shadows to each other, I talked so easy I almost didn't know myself; and she talked with me and it was as if we were two new people sprung from our old pains.

"Molly I swear I feel good times coming. The life here is working up. They'll have to cut a road to get those Concord freighters through here. And to do that they'll need lots of people, they'll have lots of jobs!"

"I hated those three. Stepping around like they was afraid to get their feetsies dirty."

"We don't have ever to see 'em again, they just came out here to make up their minds—"

"Money for their flouncy city ladies—"

"Lord, what do we care! We're going on the map!"

"You really think?"

"I know it. It's our turn."

"I am living better now than Avery ever gave me, I'll say it Blue."

"Molly I mean to make good for the three of us."

"You always fancied Flo over me."

"You were so forbidding—"

"I can't forget him. I see him in my sleep."

"If I can be alright in your eyes I'll be alright in my own."

"I keep hearing his voice: 'I'll be back,' he says. It's what he said to me."

"Well then, if that's so, I doubt it but if it's so, if he does come back then we'll be ready for him. We'll all be ready."

She was quiet for a minute. "We've both suffered," she said. And I was holding her hand in my hands. It was enough to start me keeping the books again.

No, MAYBE I'M NOT TELLING IT RIGHT. WHEN I dipped my pen in the ink it was not just for celebration, it was something that had to be done. Zar and Isaac both came to me to claim frontage on the street once they saw Jonce Early's ten-dollar gold piece. What other way was there to fix people's rights? I don't think I was such a fool as to be blinded by my feelings. We had bunks to sleep on and another room with a door, and they were good nights as we lay in one bunk, hugging like the two poor married creatures we were—she had the shyness of a bride, she was so becoming, I never knew such joy. But wasn't this time of our conjunction the time of Jimmy's dismay? And the sight of her smiles at me, like the closed door at night, a greater reason for his hate? She might waver and relent but it only fixed him more. He stayed out all the day long, I didn't see him from one meal to the next. He wouldn't talk to me and when I'd catch sight of him outside as I'd be going about my business he'd slip away fast like he hadn't heard me call. How good could it have been for two of us when there were three?

THE PAGES ARE FULL OF DEALINGS, I SEE THE ENtries, all through the year the street grew up and you can see how right here on the lines. I wrote each person's name and what he owned. I put down how Molly had all rights to me as wife and Jimmy as son. I wrote out the claims. Jonce Early came back to build a public house where he'd staked out. A smith named Roebuck figured there would be plenty of horses by and by and digging tools to fix, and so he set up his forge. Another man—I can't read his name, I never did hear him called—rode in with a wagon of coal he would sell in sacks when the winter came. More names with each passing month, I remember I marveled at it; hearing of our prospects, these people were coming to settle, it was common enough sense, but I always had the feeling somebody had certified Hard Times as a place in the world and that's why it was happening.

Here it shows how my commissions rose on the Express business. Here is the marriage notice of Bert and the little girl—he could write, but all she did was put a mark down. Now that tells a lot, the minute I began to keep the records I was the natural party to every complaint, legal or otherwise. I used to feel I was a horsebreaker and each day one of a remuda I had to cut down to size. For several Saturdays running Miss Adah, Mae and Jessie kept Bert happy by shunting only the drunkest and least able customers to the Chinese girl—so that all she had to do was lead them to a

room, take their money and leave them sleeping there.
Bert had a good length of wood near his hand while he
tended the bar and he was ready to jump out and use it
if he thought his sweetheart was having trouble. The
ladies didn't want that; and they suffered too whenever any of Bert's digging friends made a joke of him
for quitting his job at the lodes. "Like to be around the
stuff, Bert?" someone would call out—and the strain
just got to be too much for the ladies. They came to
me as a delegation and elected me to break the news
to Zar. "You can gentle him to it, Blue," Miss Adah
said, "it won't be as bad as if he finds out for himself."

So I did one day, while everyone else stayed out of
sight. Well first I had to talk Zar out of killing Bert.
And then out of firing him—that I did by convincing
him Isaac Maple would hire the boy in his place. When
I had him calmed down I said: "Look here Zar, what's
some little old Chinagirl matter when in just a few
months you'll have the finest saloon in these parts. A
businessman like you can't bother with such things."

"Not a saloon, frand. An hotel. Two stories. Glass
windows. A mirror. A polished wood bar."

"Well there you are, that's big time Zar, and big
times are coming."

"You are right."

"Sure I'm right—hell you'll be able to import a
dozen Chinese if you want, this town grows up and
you'll have more girls than you can choose."

"We will be a city!"

"Sure!"

"Alright Blue: you tell the boy I will not kill him."

"That's the decent thing, Zar."

"He loffs her, he can have her."

"Fine."

"For three hundred dollars he can have her."

Zar was a match for me, no question. When I took the news out to Bert and the others I looked at some long faces. But Molly came up with an idea: She said: "If Bert takes the girl, and brings in someone in her stead, maybe the Russian would make a trade."

So I tried that and I guess Zar didn't think there was a chance in Hell, he agreed readily. We sat there and it was like talking to some foreign king making a royal marriage for his daughter. If Bert got him another woman he wanted only one hundred dollars—which is what he'd paid for the Chinagirl—and he'd let the young fellow pay him in labor. That was all I could get out of him. He stuck to those terms for the best part of a week. Till finally Bert borrowed our mule and rig and rode off and was gone two days, and Lord! if he didn't come back with a sad grey-haired woman, full of sags, and deliver her up with a flourish. That was Mrs. Clement and I never found out where Bert got her. You just didn't look to find such enterprise in a boy like that, and part of it was the way he never told anyone how he did it.

The Russian hadn't expected Bert to come up with anyone but it was to his credit he stuck to the terms. He might even have delighted in the boy's wherewithal. But then the trouble was Mae and Jessie. They didn't take to the new woman at all, they sniffed at her and found her wanting. When Zar offered her the same arrangement he had with them they went into a rage. It was an insult to them, there was a big fuss and they made up their minds then and there to quit Zar and leave the town.

That was a noisy morning in my cabin, Jessie and Mae coming in and tearfully ordering me to write out tickets for the next stage. Miss Adah was with them, wringing her hands, and Zar shouting and ranting; and things were all inside out now as the girls were put out with Bert for disrupting things and Zar was standing up for him. But when Mae and Jessie demanded their share of the profits which Zar had been holding in trust for them, the Russian stopped the game: their money, along with his own, he had invested in the wood for the new "hotel." It was all gone, receipted by Alf, he told the furious women, and smiling he invited them to carry off their share of the lumber when it came on the freight wagons.

That took the heart out of them; and nothing more was said or done once the whole problem had reached its natural limits. By the time the lumber came, and Zar was hiring a few miners who knew how to carpenter, the women were actually looking forward to the luxury of those second-story rooms—although they never did warm up to old Mrs. Clement.

And by autumn, when the wedding was made, everyone—Zar, Mae, Jessie as well as the rest of us in the town—were happy for the two young people. And the only shadows were on the faces of Bert and his Chinagirl, both combed and clean but awful scared, and looking sorry about the whole thing.

I was the one did the marrying. I don't regret it, I think it was proper enough, it sort of fell on me to finish the business I had become party to. We stood out in front of Zar's old place. There was a scatter of people looking on including a few folks I barely knew. Over the heads, across the street, was Zar's new saloon, two stories as it was planned, with three rooms with glass windows on the second floor and a false front another story high; next to it, with an alley in between, was Isaac Maple's wood store which Swede had raised almost by himself. From where I stood the scar of the old street was blocked from my sight. None of the newcomers knew that I was no real mayor, or that the words I spoke to wed the boy and girl were those few true phrases told to me by Miss Adah—who seemed ashamed even to recall them —plus what I could summon up in my mind from the ordained minister who married me more than twenty years before. Miss Adah had a Bible too, and had offered it to me until Mae pointed out the Chinagirl wasn't hardly a Christian and so it would not be fitting.

Afterwards Zar gave out drinks on the house. His bar and his mirror weren't arrived yet and he passed the liquor out from behind his plank, we all drank up, one of the new men showed a violin, and although it was afternoon we danced around on that new pine floor till it was tolerably sanctified. Swede brought his Helga in to dance, I danced with Molly, I did alright for an old man, that rigid back was soft in my hands and there was a flush of pleasure on Molly's face as we stomped around, arms around, till we could dance no more.

Sometime between that heady evening she relented and that day we danced—there must have been a moment when we reached what perfection was left to our lives. "We've both suffered," she said, but words don't turn as the earth turns, they only have their season. When was the moment, I don't know when, with all my remembrances I can't find it; maybe it was during our dance, or it was some morning as a breeze of air shook the sun's light; maybe it was one of those nights of hugging when we reached our ripeness and the earth turned past it; maybe we were asleep. Really how life gets on is a secret, you only know your memory, and it makes its own time. The real time leads you along and you never know when it happens, the best that can be is come and gone.

WHAT MY MIND SEES NOW IS THE WINTER, November. The cabin is double-boarded, snug against the wind. Just inside, by the front door, is my desk, Swede's table which I've bought from him. There are shelves on the walls filled with provisions, pegs hung with extra boughten clothes for all of us, a commode with an ironstone jug and washbowl. Mr. Hayden Gillis sits at my desk looking a long time at my books, a man all the way from the office of the Governor of the Territory.

"What have you charged for your lots Mr. Mayor," he says shortly, turning around to face me.

"Well nothing to speak of. I put down witness stakes whenever someone claims a section he intends to build on. And he signs the ledger and I sign, that's all."

"You are not the promoter of this townsite?"

"No . . ."

"Would you believe it?" Molly says wiping her hands on her apron. "Anyone who wants, gets."

He looks from her to me—a short man with a large head, hair falling back to his shoulders, small features down near his chin. "Your records are thorough. But I see no mention of your election as mayor."

"Well no sir, I just come by the title. You see it got around how I was keeping a write on things. And then when we found there's going to be a road through us why people began to claim this piece and that along the street, and I kept things straight for them so there would be no fights. Mr. Zar, that's the Russian, and Mr. Maple the storekeep, they've been building for when the crowd comes to lay the road. Zar owns the big place down the street and the public house opposite. Isaac has the store and he's the one put up those sheet-iron cribs to rent. They are the big owners right now."

"But for this place and the windmill not a foot of streetfront do we own," Molly says angrily, "my husband likes to see other people make the money."

"Alright Molly."

"Somebody is going to drill another well, it's bound to happen although Blue doesn't see how. Then where will we be? I'll tell you Mr. Gillis, this is more than an honest man standing before you, you can trust his records for they show against him!"

"Well," the man says as he stands, "I think I've seen enough." He pulls at his hammer-claw coat, takes his stovepipe from my desk. "If you will come with me, sir," he says to me, and to Molly he nods.

Outside, although it is cold and the sky heavy, Zar and Isaac are waiting with their hats in their hands. We all four walk up to Zar's new place, not a word being said as the man strides in the lead, badly bowed in the legs and rocking with each step. Jimmy darts in from nowhere and begins to walk behind him in imitation until I take a swipe at him and he's gone again.

Isaac whispers to me: "Blue, if ye get the chance ask does he know Ezra Maple. He's a travelin' man, could be he's met my brother along the way."

I would like to ask it for Isaac, along with a few questions in my own mind, but the official is not a man who allows himself to be put upon. While the others wait at the bar we go upstairs to the room he's taken (hastily given up by Jessie the day before) and he sits down at a table by the window and works with a sheaf of papers and ink stamps for a bit, muttering to himself as if I wasn't even standing there.

"Every time someone puts a little capital into this Territory I'm called in by the Governor and sent on my way. It doesn't matter I suffer from the rheumatism, nor that I'm past the age of riding a horse's back. If a man files a claim that yields, there's a town. If he finds some grass, there's a town. Does he dig a well? Another town. Does he stop somewhere to ease his bladder, there's a town. Over this land a thousand times each year towns spring up and it appears I have to charter them all. But to what purpose? The claim pinches out, the grass dies, the well dries up, and everyone will ride off to form up again somewhere else for me to travel. Nothing fixes in this damned country, people blow around at the whiff of the wind. You can't bring the law to a bunch of rocks, you can't settle the coyotes, you can't make a society out of sand. I sometimes think we're worse than the Indians.... What is the name of this place, Hard Times? You are a well-meaning man Mr. Blue, I come across your likes occasionally. I noticed Blackstone on your desk, and Chitty's Pleadings. Well you can read the law as much as you like but it will be no weapon for the spring when the town swells with people coming to work your road. You need a peace officer but I don't even see you wearing a gun. I look out of this window and I see cabins, loghouse, cribs, tent, shanty, but I don't see a jail. You'd better build a jail. You'd better find a shootist and build a jail."

Then he turns and goes to his Gladstone traveling bag, unlocks it, burrows under some things and comes up with a labeled bottle of whiskey and two small glasses. He rubs the glasses with the flap of his coat, and then glancing up at me with that small face in that big head he hands me a glass and pours: "The jail can wait, but now let's drink to the end of your tenure."

Well everything he's said I stow in my mind, only thinking now what his visit means: it will be a long year of expectations but by the spring they will come true.

I don't remember tasting whiskey as good as that. A few minutes later I walked down the stairs while the anxious faces looked up at me from the bar: Zar, Isaac, Swede, Bert Albany—none of them would do. Before anyone could say anything I went out and up the street to the stable and found Jenks sleeping just inside the door. I shook him awake and dragged him back to Hayden Gillis. And at the top of the stairs, while everyone below looked on amazed, and while Jenks himself stood wide awake now with his mouth open the man stuck a tin star on his jacket and swore him in as a Deputy Sheriff, salary twenty-five dollars a year payable the following year.

"You ever kill your man?" Mr. Gillis asked Jenks.

Jenks turned red: "Yessir, reckon . . ."

"Good. You're running this town now. See to it these folks make up a pot for a jailhouse. Get the records from Mr. Blue here and keep them neat. First time you get a serious outlaw, undead, write a letter to the capital and we'll put a circuit judge on to you. Here's paper. Town charter. Census list forms. Petition for statehood you can get people to sign when there's nothing else to keep you busy."

Then the man was clumping downstairs with his bag in his hand and his stovepipe hat and out the doors he went without a nod to anyone. Isaac Maple called up to me: "Blue?" But I shrugged and he ran out after.

Everyone else crowded around me at the bar. What did it come to, this man's visit? What was happening? I smiled because there could be no doubt. "Rest your mind Zar," I said to the Russian, "all the money you're in for will come back at you double."

Jenks, in the meantime, was standing on the stairs with that sheaf of papers in his hand, glancing down at the badge on his coat and then toward the doors and back again at his chest. He was well confounded. But then he began to appreciate what had happened and as he came down each step his wolfy smile got wider and wider.

"Wall," Zar shouted, "we are OK and without worry now Janks is Sheriff!"

Everyone laughed. Jenks came up to the bar and said to Bert who was tending: "Somethin' fer everman heah!" and he waved his hand grandly. In the drinking that followed Jenks laid his papers on the bar. They must have fallen off in the fun, I found them later on the floor, bootmarks all over them. I gathered them up and tucked them inside my vest.

JENKS'S BEING A LAWMAN DIDN'T CHANGE THINGS much. People still came to me with what was on their minds; and I still kept the ledgers. I was ready to give them to him any time he asked. But maybe a month after Hayden Gillis had been through, the Sheriff came to me saying as he'd allow me to do the paperwork for him considering how busy he was on the street keeping an eye on matters—and how, besides, I knew how to write. And from then, as before, he had no part in anything that was on my desk, except to come in once or twice each day to look over my shoulder if I was sitting there, to nod sagely, but more likely only to get a free meal from Molly. So far as I know nobody in the town paid Jenks much attention except to make a joke of him now and then; but Molly and Jimmy treated him with respect and deference and it made him feel more the man he was supposed to be. He paced the street regular, wearing a gun in an open holster from his belt, and his star carefully displayed. And sometimes Jimmy followed a few steps after him and it got so you could tell where Jenks was by spotting Jimmy at some door along the street.

By the new year the street ran from my cabin, which was its southernmost end, in a crescent that found itself once more at John Bear's shack at the foot of the trail leading up to the lodes. It was a full year, and half again another, since the day I put spade to earth for a dugout.

Molly said: "All these fools have come like buzzards after the smell of meat."

"Buzzards eat what's dead, Molly. This town is alive."

"Nobody talks. They're all keeping an eye out."

"They're waiting for the spring, Molly." Why did I need to tell her so? "Everyone stands to make a little money comes the warm weather."

"Jimmy?" she called.

We were by the front of our door in the dark of late afternoon. There was a crust of snow on the ground. Up the street there were lights shining from the windows. In the sharp, cold air, you could smell suppers cooking.

"Molly," I turned to her, "what's worrying you? We are alright, can't you see that? We are prospering."

Just then Jimmy jumped out of the shadows where

we hadn't been looking for him. He put his hands over Molly's eyes: "Hoo!" he said in her ear.

She started. Then she pulled him around to her and held him tight: "Oh Mayor," she said, "if this town stretched four ways as far as the eye could see, it would still be a wilderness!"

The boy's trick had startled me too. And for one chilling moment I knew what Molly meant. A shudder ran down my back. But then the true sight of our town returned to me, and once more Molly and I were looking at the same scene but with different eyes. I had to smile how like a woman it was to scare in the good times.

That was only last winter but it seems like ancient days in my mind.

THIRD
LEDGER

TEN

I HAVE BEEN TRYING TO WRITE WHAT HAPPENED but it is hard, wishful work. Time is beginning to run out on me, and the form remembrance puts on things is making its own time and guiding my pen in ways I don't trust. In my mind's eyes is an arch of suns multiplying the sky—or a long flickering night of one moon turning over and over into its shadows. I know this is trickery but I can't blot it out. I think Molly, Molly, Molly and she is the time, turning in her phases like that moon, smiling and frowning while the boy grows big, setting down in frame like Fee his father. ... And I see something that never happened, the two of them carrying a giant cross with great effort, planting it over Fee. "I ain't much for God," he protests, "I always put my faith in people."

Molly, could you really know what was coming? Or did it come because you knew it? Were you smarter than the life, or did the life depend on you?

There was a sign they put up when the weather grew warm. Isaac provided a bolt of muslin and Zar bought the paint; and young Bert spent a week painting the red letters in the style he copied out of a catalogue. Helga sewed on a canvas backing, making slits against the wind. And on a dazzling morning Swede raised up the sign over the street. From the scaffold of the well it stretched all the way across to the false front of Zar's saloon: WELCOME TO HARD TIMES, it said, rippling in the breeze like a thing alive.

Most everyone stood outside for the occasion, gazing up at the banner and making comment. I figured you could see that sign half a mile away on the flats. But that was the morning Molly broke down crying and said: "Blue, for God's sake let's leave this place!"

And then, for some weeks, not a day passed and she didn't say it again, begging, pleading with me to sell out: "It's not safe any more, I swear we've got to get out of here!"

"Where do you want to go Molly?"

"Christ, I don't know. Let's just leave, Blue. Right now. Today. The three of us, we'll find somewhere—"

"Molly what you're saying makes no sense. Here we've put all this work, and life down, we've made a home from nothing, and you want to ride off!"

"God, you're a fool, Mayor. You always was a fool!"

"That may be. But I'm not fool enough to pull up stakes just when the claim is beginning to pay! You don't think it's different anywhere else do you? You don't think there's only one Turner riding this land!"

"Oh Christ there are hundreds, yes I know. Thousands. And they're going to get me—they're all coming for me!"

If I was a wiser man I would have seen where the misery was. You could step out the door and the scar of the old town was blocked from your sight, but the scar was still there.

"I suppose you'll protect me! I suppose you'll take care of me, just like the last time. Good old Mayor, fast with the gun he is, no worries with Mayor Blue marching behind your skirts. No worries at all!"

And there would be that hand closing over my heart, that almost forgotten pain.

"Why these fools, with their banners and their shacks, and their big plans—Oh God, we've got to get away from here!"

"Molly please—"

I would hold her in my arms and she would weep with great sobs that made her shudder: "Blue—I beg you—sell out—and we'll go—to some city—Blue." I would touch her hair, press her head to my chest and stand with her until she was quietened. I remember once how I sat her down at the table. Her green eyes were puffed with crying as she leaned on her elbow, her head in her hand, trying to listen to me.

"Molly, it could be you are right and this street in all its bustle will bring some Bad Man. I'll say you are right—sure as winter brings summer we'll draw our Man from Bodie. I suppose I know it as well as you. But you see this time we'll be too good for him. Listen to what I say: I don't mean I'll stand up to his gun, I mean I won't have to. When he came last time, the minute Flo walked over to him we were lost. Before Fee went in Avery's place with his stick of wood we were lost. You fight them, you just look at them, and they have you. Molly it's something I know, I've seen enough, I've seen them ride into a town, a bunch of them, feeling out the place, prodding for the right welcome. And when they get it you'd might as well turn your gun on yourself as try to turn them away. But a settled town drives them away. When the business is good and the life is working they can't do a thing, they're destroyed."

"Oh Lord," she wailed, "oh Jesus God, spare me from this man, this talker—"

"Molly! You know something? Listen to me, you know why he came that time? *We wanted him.* Our tongues were just hanging out for him. Even poor old Fee, he built a street but he couldn't make a proper town. He must have knowed when he picked up that board the hope was already dead. If he didn't know he wasn't the man I think he was; if he was fooled he couldn't know what life is."

"Blue—"

"Molly, if you believe me, believe what I'm saying, and that Turner will never get to us!"

AFTER A WHILE SHE DIDN'T ASK IT ANY MORE. That in itself should have made me pack and ride us out. It was not from any comfort I supplied that she spoke no more of leaving; but from what, I think now, was a giving-in to the devil that grinned at her. Weren't those cries—"I beg you Blue, please Blue, Blue Blue Blue"—weren't they cries for help? I was no help, once more I was walking her to the saloon, behind her still.

It was as if she grudged anyone's life who hadn't suffered at the hands of that Bad Man. When people began to ride in under the banner she grew sullen. One day she fastened two sticks together for a cross and with Jimmy went out to the graves to put it at Fee's head. I watched them from the cabin door, and I remembered the order of those graves: they were planting the cross, by mistake, for one-armed Jack Millay.

She would take no part in the life on the street, she began to stay inside, only sitting sometimes out in back when the weather was fair, looking at the view west of the rocks and the flats. I did the buying for us and

Jimmy brought her the news. He was good at that, always managing to be where something was going on; and then he'd run to Molly to tell her about it. In that way she had all the news; and Jimmy had all her opinions. Molly's opinions were much the same about everything. Whether it was someone come on the stage, or some rumor about the road, some new business of Zar's or Isaac Maple's, or some measure I had taken—she didn't like it. Everything fell under her tongue and there would be suppers where I would eat while Molly would talk on and on, her mind wandering over each person, each foot of ground, and I'd be finished and my coffee drunk and her plate would hardly be touched. Jimmy listened to everything she said like it was gospel, no matter what she spoke of or how many times she'd said it before, he would drink up her words like they were mother's milk.

There was only one person who Molly would tolerate and that was Jenks—not because he was anything but a fool but because he was so handy with guns. Jenks's name never felt the whip at our table and that was why he was one of the few people Jimmy had a talking acquaintance with. Many's the time I saw the boy helping Jenks at the stable, mucking out stalls, running errands. For pay Jimmy got to coddle the animals, and sometimes the boon of a lesson in gun handling. I found him at it once, holding a Colt shoulder-high, clicking off the trigger at the barn walls while Jenks held a stick under his wrist and ran a patter: "Hold 'm steady, sonny, squeeze 'm, squeeze 'm, don't yer pull, thet's hit, line 'm steady. . . . " I tried to put a stop to it and that's when I found out Jenks was teaching the boy just to oblige Molly, who had asked him the favor.

Now there is no wrong in showing a boy arms except it was like everything else Jimmy was getting. And the effect of it all wasn't lost on other people. He was thickening into his father's son but the look on his face was Molly's. Mae told me privately, because she didn't want to make any fuss she said, that she greeted the boy one day looking out her second-story window, and in a sudden rage he picked up a stone and threw it right up, hitting her in the chest. Isaac Maple caught him once pocketing a handful of shells from the counter. I settled with Isaac but it wasn't the money that bothered him. And there was no settling at all with John Bear: the Indian's garden patch was more than food to him, there was no one else who could make a plant grow. But one day he woke from his nooning and there was his greens all stepped on. He never thought of Jimmy, for some reason he made me understand it was Zar he blamed—unlikely as Zar would be to do such a thing. But I knew who it was. And I thought it wouldn't do to talk to him or lay a hand to him. I thought it was Molly who needed reaching.

"Molly that boy gets wilder each day. He's turning mean."

"Is that what you think?"

"He threw a rock at Mae."

"Well I hope it was thrown true."

"Molly this is Fee's boy—"

"I'll tell you what's rankling you Mayor, he's a fondness for Jenks, he looks up to Jenks. And it burns don't it?"

"Jenks has nothing to do with it!"

"Were you any good with a gun, Mayor, maybe you could teach the boy some manliness."

"That's not manliness."

"Oh I'll tell you it is, it is, Mayor—"

"Well is it manliness to step all over the Indian's patch?"

She looked at me. Then she went to the door and called the boy and a moment later Jimmy came inside and stood in front of her.

"Was it you ruffled up those plants?"

The boy glanced at me with a disgusted look on his face: "No."

"Was it?" Molly grabbed his shoulders and shook him and he went scared: "Yes ma'am."

One two three she put the slaps smart across his face.

"You do such as that again, I'll have your hide. You hear me?" She screamed: "You hear me?"

Well that wasn't what I wanted either, I could have hurt him myself if it would serve the purpose. As it was he hated me as he fingered the slaps Molly gave him. A night or so later I found my ink jar turned over and the cover of one of the ledgers all soaked. It riled me and I was ready to forget anything but my own anger and light into the boy no matter what purpose it would serve. But as I turned there was Molly in the dugout, his room now, watching the boy get ready for bed.

"Look at them shoulders," I listened to her murmur. "Molly's Jim is gettin' tall and strong, ain't he? Molly feeds him up good and he's turning into a sure enough man, isn't it so? Big Jim they'll call him and he'll take care of his Molly, yes he will. . . ."

THIS WAS THE TIME OF OUR GREATEST PROSPERITY. Small clouds of gnats hung in the yellow evenings and horses tied up to the porch rails were touching rumps.

Every rising sun saw another cone of dust sprouting up from the flats. People needed work; and it was like all the West was following the smell of it on the spring airs, like the scent of water on the desert. What were my feelings, did it make me uneasy to see our town as a refuge? How many times I would open the door to see wheels turning past us: it was a dusty couple pulling hard on their handcart, or a Pike County bunch filling a flatbed wagon, one limping beside with his kneecoat and Bowie belt, an old long rifle on his shoulders. You could tell the Pike Counties if only by their coughs. A man rode in one day wearing a dirty white linen suit, a roll of green felt was across his saddle, he was a faro dealer. And there was much bidding between Zar and Jonce Early to get the man. Zar got him. There was a raggedy old woman come along, nothing in her wagon but a pile of rags and a crate with three squawking chickens; and she made money selling their eggs for a dollar apiece. But most of the arrivals had just themselves to offer a boss and the money was going into the pockets mainly of those already settled on the street.

We were all doing a brisk business. People paid in every kind of exchange for my water—U.S. silver, greenbacks, Territory scrip; and when I wasn't busy seeing to the well I was noting Express orders and taking mail. There was another stage on the line now and we had two arrivals each week. If you went into Isaac Maple's store ("Maple Bros." it said on the outside in paint, Isaac's hope lettered for all to see), if you went in there, there was always someone ahead of you—even though Isaac had the Chinagirl helping him wait on customers. The store had every kind of stock you could wish; sugar, flour, foods canned and in brine barrels, preserves, dry goods, cutlery, carpentry tools, tar paper, rolls of barbed wire, tobaccos, anquitum for lice, corn starch, bottled lavender water and honey and castor oil—you'd think you was in Silver City.

Directly across from the store, every morning and evening, there was always a crowd in front of the tent, which Swede rented now for his eatery. They would stand there waiting for the big fellow to let them in. For twenty-five cents you could eat a breakfast of flourcakes and coffee, for fifty cents a dinner of salt pork, coffee and biscuits made up by Helga. I ate there myself once Molly stopped cooking.

As for the Russian he couldn't ask for better business, even with his competition across the street. Whenever someone rode in it was usually to "Zar's Palace" he went for information, since it was the tallest building in the town. Bert, behind the fancy bar over there, would send them to my door; or if it was Swede in his restaurant, he would wipe his big hands on his apron and lead the stranger over to me. There was nobody from the mine set up in the town as yet and so I kept a list of all those who wanted work. I didn't state myself as an agent for the mine, in fact I was always sure to make it clear I wasn't; but it helped me to know who was in town and besides I was able to use the chance to get another signature on the petition for statehood. And it always gave the stranger a feeling of having done all he could do until the hiring began, to write his name down. I must have had a half a hundred names on that list.

ONE DAY I CAME BACK TO THE CABIN IN THE evening and there was no fire on the stove or supper on the table. Then she stopped doing laundry. And then I was the one sweeping dust, every morning, every night. The load gets heavier and you shift to it, that's all, you can accommodate yourself without even realizing.

A man came up to me in front of Swede's tent and said: "Mayor I was just by your place to post a letter but nobody answered the knock."

"My wife's always home," I said.

"Well yes, and I saw smoke from your chimney pipe, the Mrs. Mayor hard of hearin'?" He grinned at me.

"Give me your letter," I said, "I'll take it now."

I went down the street. It was a warm day and no wind blew. A heavy stench of life filled the air, flies stuck to your clothes and you had to rub the gnats off your face.

"Molly!" The door was latched and I banged it and banged it until she let me in.

"Listen," I said, "you've got to stop this!"

"I don't want filth in my house."

"You think everyone knocks is the Man from Bodie?"

"Keep away from me!"

"People come to me with business, you run in the dugout. Someone wipes his feet and takes his hat off and you curse him!"

"Every manner of filth and dirt, every tramp, every stinking lowlife!"

"You are getting a name in this town, Molly. I don't like you acting this way!"

"Get out then! They're all like you. All the filth. They're no worse than you are, damn you!" And she ran into the back room and slammed the door.

That was the way she was acting. It was as if each person coming into town was taking away a little more of her air to breathe. What could I do? I see now what was going on but can I say I saw then?

Jimmy accepted her disposition, it should have bothered him that she began to ignore him most of the time, but he saw her only a certain way and he was rewarded whenever she came back to him with a rush of feeling. He kept up his duties to her like a faith. For instance people knowing who he was would sometimes give him their dollars for the water. I was keeping no strict records on such payments, but I knew he turned over to Molly as much money as he ever gave into my hands. Where she hid it I didn't know, or what she wanted to do with it. I knew she wasn't making plans to leave, she was past making plans for her life, if I could have foreseen I would have put her on the stage myself, I would have bought her a catalogue dress and bonnet and packed her a satchel of greenbacks saying Go on Molly, you were right and I was wrong, the look of your cat's green eyes will stay with me, go as far as this money takes you and leave Hard Times to the Mayor. . . .

But one night I found out where the money went.

"Blue." Her whisper coming across the room. "Blue, you sleeping?"

"No."

"Why aren't you sleeping? What's on your mind, Blue, that you can't sleep?"

"Nothing."

"Tell me. Tell Molly your trouble."

"What?"

"You want to come over here, you want to come to your Molly? Alright. Alright." I heard her moving in her bed, making room for me.

"I was just thinking of that letter come for Archie

D. Brogan," I said quickly. I didn't know what had got into her.

"He's got a letter?"

"A letter addressed with a typewriting machine. I wish I knew what it said, that's all."

A giggle: "Well you fool, why don't you open it?"

"Go to sleep Molly."

"Come here Blue. Come give me a hug and forget that letter you say is worrying you out of your sleep. It's not any letter is it? You know what it is, come on, come to your Molly."

I had not thought of her that way for how long? How long had it been since she turned, little by little, so compliant, that I felt I was some duplicate Bad Man taking his pleasure?

"I want to whisper something. I really have to tell something in your ear—"

I am a foolish man, I shall always have to go to Molly when she calls, knowing everything, expecting anything, I will still go. I put my feet over the side of the bunk and she cried, "JIMMY!" Loud enough to wake the town, "JIMMY!" she screamed.

And there at the door, the dim light of the cabin behind him, he stood torn out of his sleep and a shotgun cradled in his arm, the boy.

"You'll keep away from me now Mayor? You'll stay away? You try to touch me and you see what'll happen to you? You see you lechering old bastard!" And that was her voice I recognized.

With a groan I was at the boy, wrestling the gun from him. He was half asleep, he stumbled over to her bed and fell into her arms, making sounds like he was shivering. "There, it's alright Jim, Molly's alright, don't you fret—" I took his arm and I pulled him away. "Go on to your bed," I swung him past me, "go on or I'll whip you good!" I herded him all the way back to his cot, shoving him so that he fell down the step into the dugout. "Oh oww!" he cried, rubbing his toes, and I left him sitting there and crying.

That new oily double-barrel glinting blue was in my hands and I swung it like a hammer against my desk but the stock didn't break. Through the door there was Molly sitting up, holding the blanket up to her neck, her hair was down and she was giggling at her joke, the laughter came out of her closed mouth in fits. I threw the gun at her. It hit the wall and fell behind her. She stopped laughing, her mouth set in a prim smile, righteous and suffering, and that was the face I slammed the door on.

I sat down and held my head in my hands. How could one man have been so blind stupid in his life! God help me for my sight, my heart went out to this child. Was everything, even her old sweetness to me, a design on him? She was training him for the Bad Man, she was breaking him into a proper mount for her own ride to Hell, and I hadn't seen it till now, I hadn't ever understood it was not me who suffered her, it was Jimmy.

WHEN IT WAS DECENTLY DAY I WENT OVER TO Zar's place. "Pour you a breakfast Mayor?" Mae said quietly when I stepped through the doors. "You look as you could use it."

The place was mostly empty, a few people were sleeping at the tables. The night air was still in the room, it was cool but it smelled bad.

"Bert not here yet?" I said.

"Can't expeck him to leave a cozy bed jes' cause he has a job to do," she said, pouring, "can't expeck him to leave his Chink honey."

I took my drink.

"'Smatter, Blue, that wife o' yourn givin' ye a time?"

"What?"

"Man looks like you do in the mornin', either it's his wife or his liver. Ain't got no liver trouble so far as I know."

"You don't look so good yourself," I said. She had no color in her face, she was not so plump any more. "You not enjoying the prosperity, Mae?"

"What do you want, Mayor, goddamnit." She was rubbing her forehead. "Don't know what it's like to breathe any more. Used to be jes' the week's end, these days every night is Saturday."

Zar came clumping down the stairs. He dressed fancy now. "La la la," he was singing, he came over and pinched Mae's cheek. "Maechka," he said, but she pushed his hand off and went to sit down with her glass.

"Blue," the Russian turned smiling to me, "you are the man I am meaning to see. I have important business to talk."

"Not now Zar."

"Of course now. You have just to listen." He carefully took from his pocket a folded piece of newspaper. "At Silver City I see there is Company, for three hundred dollars they will go anywhere with steam drill and dig the water."

"So?"

"So I tell you and you won't be mad. I am thinking closely of sending for them. That way I have my own well."

"Congratulations."

"But not to sell water to others, I promise you that."

Mae laughed. He turned and glared at her.

"Zar," I said, "do what you want. But the minute you put up a well Isaac Maple will too. You know that don't you?"

He shrugged. "What do I care?"

"Well then why should you think I care what you do? Do what you want and good luck to you." A couple of men walked in the doors and then a few more after them. The day was beginning. I put money on the bar and I walked out.

On the porch a man stepped in front of me: "Mornin' Mayor," he mumbled, "jest wonderin' is there any news—"

"You'll know when I know," I said shortly.

"I know Mayor but I can't—"

"Come over to my place when I'm there," I said. "I got other business just now."

Isaac was on his porch, putting out some wares, I went inside with him and spoke to him for a few minutes. When I was through I went down the street to the cabin. Molly was in the room behind the door and she was asleep, but the dugout was empty.

It was toward the middle of the morning but hot and still enough for afternoon. A few men were walking out of Swede's tent and they were picking their teeth. I went up there and Swede was just coming out carrying a pair of kettles.

"I'm looking for my boy," I said.

"Ya," he smiled, "inside."

Jimmy was not at any of the long tables. A dozen heads glanced up as I looked around. I found him out in back, cross-legged on the ground, rolling pancakes and stuffing them in his mouth. He wouldn't look at me. Swede's wife was standing by him, her hands in her apron, smiling as she watched him eat.

"Jimmy you'll come with me," I said.

I dug in my pockets to pay for his breakfast but Helga shook her head and waved my hand down. When he was finished I walked away without looking back. I went down the street past Bear's shack, getting on the trail and climbing up. I was feeling short of breath but I kept up my pace and turned off well along the trail, when I saw a flat rock. I picked my way to it and sat down and waited for him. And a minute later he came along and stood a few feet away looking at me.

"Sit down here," I said, "I've got something to say to you." He didn't move. "I won't hurt you, come on."

We sat side by side watching the town below us, a street of houses at the foot of that vast flatland, a small stir of life in all that stillness. A cool breeze blew on the face but down there it wasn't enough to turn the windmill. Horses and mules were tied up along the railings, people were walking this way and that, every now and then a fragment of someone's voice would rise up to our ears, or something would catch the sun and flash in our eyes.

"I brought you up here because I wanted to be sure no one would bother us," I said. "What I have to say is private between you and me. You understand that?"

"Sure."

"How old do you reckon you are? Fourteen? Fifteen years?"

"I don't know."

"You're a sight bigger than the day I carried you down from these rocks. You remember that? You took my gun, you were going after that Bad Man killed your Daddy."

My gaze went out beyond the town to the graves in the flats, and I suppose he looked there too. I didn't dare look at him, I didn't trust myself to say just what I wanted to say.

"You remember that?"

"Yes."

"I don't think I could carry you now. I don't suppose if you didn't want it I could make you do anything. But I'll tell you: When I got you down to the Indian's shack I put you down too fast. I let you go too quick. I should have made plans for you then and there. But I never had practice being a father before and I didn't know any better."

I felt him looking at me but I kept my own eyes on the town. "Now look at down there. It's not as neat as the town Fee put up, it don't show one man's mark. Just a patch job, spit and old lumber but if he could see it he'd like it. He'd say it was alright."

"How do you know what my Pa would say!"

"I used to talk to him. I know what he valued. He died two years short, it would have pleasured him to see this."

He picked up a stone and tossed it away, watching it bounce down among the rocks.

"Now when he died I said to myself, 'Well he has left a son and I'm going to look after his son and pass on the lesson I learned from Fee.' It's not something a person could learn in one day or one week. It's something you have to learn *into*, like carpentry. You understand?"

He said nothing.

"And I knew that, so I never said a word to you. I figured if I did as your father did why that would be the way; if I did everything as Fee would have done it, well you'd learn alright. And you mightn't suffer the loss so bad."

Down below a woman was filling her buckets at the water tank. A man, it looked like Jenks, was walking into Zar's Palace.

"Course I was wrong, I should have taken you in hand right away and talked to you as I am now. Molly has got to you, it's natural I suppose, but if you grow to the life the way she has, I'm saying it clear as I can Jimmy, you won't have the idea, you won't be Fee's son any more."

"What do you know—"

"You've got to allow for Molly. She can't give up her suffering."

"My Pa had sand. He weren't no coward."

"Does she call me that? Well now I've got to tell you"—looking at him, feeling the desperation of what I was doing—"probably your Pa did only one shameful thing in his life and that was to rush in after Turner."

"What?"

"That was the one time he was no example to you. He went in there to get himself killed."

"What?"

"It's what you do when a Bad Man comes, Jimmy. I tried to do it too but I am a bumbler by nature."

"You better not talk that way about my Pa—" Lord, it made me faint-hearted, it was Fee's face with no lines, a young hairless face with a frown of anger and no understanding at all. "You better not talk that way," it said pursing its lips, "you better not!"

And what did I expect, you can't tell something like that, who will know it? "Jim you can squeeze the trigger and knock down a Bad Man and as sure as you've been shootin', another will come up in his place. They take to this land, they don't need much to grow, just a few folks together will breed 'em, a little noise and they'll spring up out of the empty shells. Jimmy!"

He had jumped up. Molly was stepping out of the cabin, a small figure in the street below.

"I have spoken to Isaac Maple," I said trying to control my voice. "Isaac will need someone to help him out before long. The Chinagirl is getting too heavy to move around, her time is coming. What do you say to working in Isaac's store? It will be good for you. You're going to work regular hours. You're going to learn reading and writing. You're going to grow up proper with this town and the day will come—"

"She's calling me! Here!" He waved his arms. "I'm here!"

I pulled him down. I took hold of his shoulders and held him down on the rocks. "What kind of a mama's boy are you! How far do I have to take you to get you out of that woman's spell! Listen to me I said the day is coming when no Man from Bodie will ride in but he'll wither and dry up to dust. You hear me? I'm going to see you grow up with your own mind, I'm going to see you settled just like this town, you're going to be a proper man and not some saddle fool wandering around with his grudge. Jimmy listen to me—"

He was struggling under me, a strong boy, not hearing, his face screwed up in hate. And I felt his breath clean as grass on my face and I talked on and on as if words could do something. "Listen listen," I kept saying but the strength was draining out of me, like hope, and my mind was doing another talking: It's too late, and I've done it wrong, I am too late.

He pushed me over and jumped up and delivered a kick in my side and ran off down the trail. It was a powerful kick and well aimed, I feel it now on a deep breath. Below in the town there was no sign of Molly.

But as I sat up and looked I could hear a clatter somewhere and a moment later out of the tent two skirted
figures stumbled into the sun, locked together. Someone shouted and people were running from all direc-
tions, pouring out of the saloon, the store, to make up
a circle around those two. Another moment and I saw
Jimmy arrive, ducking into the crowd.

It was Molly rolling around in the dirt with Swede's
wife Helga. Molly had made up her mind to take af-
front because the woman had been feeding up her boy.
As I ran down I could hear people yelling encourage-
ment. But by the time I made my way through the
circle Jenks and Swede had pulled the two women
apart. They stood glaring, wild-haired and gasping,
scratched and mussed so you could hardly tell one
from the other. Molly's dress was torn in front. "Lookit thet tit," a man said.

Later I stood in the cabin holding a hand to my side,
watching the boy bathe her scalp where Helga had
pulled out the hair. Molly was moaning on her bed.
There was a knock at the door and it was Swede,
wringing his hands. Behind him, down the street, was
the sound of his ranting wife.

"Blue, dis is a bad tang, my vault, forgive my Helga, my vault—"

"You big dumb stupid Swede!" I shouted. I could
feel the water come to my eyes. How was it his fault?
What in Hell made him think he must take the blame?

ELEVEN

I SAY THAT WAS THE TRUE END OF ME NO MATTER what happened after. Sharp as the boy's kick in my side, clear as the pain, was the sudden breathless vision I had of my unending futility. Who as well as I and what I am could have ensured the one's madness and the other's corruption? But we won't think about it: I tried to keep my heart by taking it out of doors. And how long was I able to do that? One week? One hour?

Some of these spring-comers paid for lodging and moved into one of Isaac Maple's cribs. And there was cabin space for those willing to share beds. But the town wasn't big enough to take on everyone and nobody was doing any more building. Those who had the money to build were making it too easily in other ways. "Who cares where they stay," Zar said to me, "they are drinking my whiskey, they are bouncing in my beds!" So after a while there were squatters staked out in back of the buildings, living out of their wagons, lying down for the night under lean-tos. And it began to make trouble.

I mean people would throw their slops into the alleys. Some didn't care where they did their business and it got so you were hard put to walk in the street without putting your boot down in a mess. One morning Molly found a drunken man peeing against the door, and it drove her to distraction, she cried the whole day. I tried to call a meeting at the well of all the people who owned streetfront, some of them had privies in back, but not all; but only Jenks and Isaac and Swede came. Jenks said: "Jes watch yer step in all yer do. Hit's good fer the land. How do the Indian get his greens up if not by shittin' on 'em all winter?" Isaac was righteous: "Nobody cares a damn," he said, "but if they all come up with dysentery 'tain't themselves they'll blame but each other." Isaac had the right sentiment but he was a busy man. It was Swede and I who ended up digging and fencing sumps behind each side of the street. That Swede would do anything you asked of him, he would tilt his head away from his wen and close his eyes and nod yes—no matter what it was.

Well the sumps helped but not much. And there were other troubles too. A few of the job hunters were men not easy to look at, there was one fellow who had running sores all over his face, another, an old man, who was humpbacked with hands twisted and swollen out of shape. Isaac came to me claiming whenever one such came into his store everyone else cleared out and he lost business. It was not true, of course, he just wanted me to run these people out of town. "Speak to Jenks," I told him, "Jenks is the peace officer here." Then Zar joined the protest, he refused to serve the hunchbacky one day and the man, in resentment, ran over to Mae and Jessie and waved his crippled hands in front of their eyes. Zar told Bert to throw the poor fellow out but Bert wouldn't step out from behind the bar. The Russian came running to me and I told him he'd best serve the man his drink and he'd leave then twice as fast and with no trouble. "It's easier in the end," I said. But Zar like Isaac was for running these people off and Jenks finally rounded up three or four of them at gunpoint and shooed them away into the flats; but at night they were back, they wanted work like everyone, and for a while they made their way behind houses and took their meals behind Swede's tent from what Helga handed out to them through the flap. And after a while they came into the store again and the saloons and so the trouble was not ended but in fact greater, with greater hard feelings.

One morning the egg lady found one of her three chickens with its head wrung off; she was an oldtimer in the West and she told her sorrows to nobody, but grabbed up her cane and went into Zar's Palace swinging. She must have been a teetotaler to blame only the whiskey for her lost hen, she bruised a number of shoulders and broke some bottles and a row of glasses Zar had proudly imported from the East before she was finally herded out; and that was my problem too because I was the one who had to gentle her.

The weather was getting hotter; and each morning of prosperity that would start out fresh and easy to breathe was turning into a day more hot and burdensome than the last. Every time Alf's stage came in, or a freight wagon, all I wanted to see was some Eastern engineer, a man in black, with plans in his pocket and wagers to give out. On Saturday night with the miners pouring in the town and the street filling with the noise of frolic from one end to the other I found Angus Mcellhenny lighting up his pipe in front of the stable.

"If the Company is going to lay a road," I asked him, "why in hell don't they start in?"

"Blue it's many years I've been diggin' the earth and I've seen fortunes in my shovel. But I've nought to show for it but my calluses and m' mind is as weak as it ever was. I dinna know."

"Well what do you hear around Angus?"

"Don't pry at me my ferlie friend. I know nothin'. We are diggin' hard six days o' the week and keepin' our eyes on the ground. I can tell you no more."

"Alright Angus. But tell Archie D. Brogan when you see him there's a letter in his name down here."

He took the pipe from his mouth: "Who from?"

"It doesn't say, Angus, it's only his name on the front. You'll tell him?"

He nodded and walked away.

It baffled me that Angus should be so close-mouthed, it wasn't like him. Meanwhile the same questions I had put to him were being asked of other miners and none of them liked it, the hungry looks in the eyes of the towners didn't go well with them. Some newcomers, not happy about waiting around, had gone up the trail looking for work at the lodes; and though they had ridden back, sour-faced, the same day, it didn't sit well with the diggers that a lot of men were in the country wanting jobs. There was no love lost between the two groups that Saturday night. The miners, having their pay to spend, sort of took over at the saloons. One thing led to another and Jenks was kept fairly busy breaking up scuffles, once or twice he even had to draw his pistol to get things quiet. In our cabin I was at the desk trying to put some order in all my papers, and Molly sat with sewing on her lap, and we heard clearly the screeches of the ladies over at Zar's every time a fight started. Molly's hands shook so she couldn't work the needle, she dropped her hands in her lap and I saw out of the corner of my eye how frightened she was. Every few minutes Jimmy would come rushing in to tell of the latest fuss, sweat on his forehead and such joy in his eyes he could hardly speak without stammering: "Old J-Jenks, he took care of 'm alright, socked 'm on the head, poom, like th- that—"

"Jimmy," I said, "you stay in here now, go on to bed, it's late. You hear me, son?" But he would never hear me.

He gave one glance to Molly and ran out, leaving the door open wide.

She made no move to stop him, sitting there her eyes fixed on nothing, one hand on her throat's cross, the other knuckled against her teeth.

A DAY OR TWO LATER AND THE SUN NOT EVEN up, Bert Albany rapped on the door until I heard him, and with the sleep still in my eyes I went with him up the street to Zar's place. The faro dealer was lying on the floor there, ashen white, and a big red rent in his vest where he had been stabbed. Jenks was standing nearby, clutching the collar of that little hunchback, his gun was drawn and sticking in the man's back. Bert told me the faro dealer had been lending out money to people at high rates, sometimes winning it back at his table. He had a list, Bert saw it, of the men indebted to him. The hunchbacky had been sitting there losing all of his loan, and when it was gone he jumped up and stuck a knife in the dealer's belly.

The dealer was quiet, concentrating on his breathing, he was in his senses enough to know to lay still. I went out to John Bear's shack. It showed even then the signs of resentment, the door was splintered, a board or two was gone from the roof. I woke the Indian up and gave him to understand there was someone needed doctoring. He came with me up to the saloon but when he saw it was Zar's place and the Russian waiting at the door, he turned on his heel and went back the way he came.

Zar and I carried the dealer up to one of the rooms, Zar being careful every step not to get any of the man's blood on his clothes. Miss Adah, with her hair in braids and a shawl over her nightdress, said she'd sit with the man and see what she could do.

When I came back down the stairs Jenks and his prisoner were gone, the few people who had watched the goings-on had drifted away. Zar offered me a drink but there wasn't anything I wanted less. Outside was the sound of hammering, and from the porch, in the grey light, I saw Jenks in the front of his stable. He had put the hunchback in Hausenfield's old boarded-up hearse wagon and was nailing the door shut.

"Jenks," I went over to him, "what in God's name are you doing!"

"Hit'll do fer a jail, don't ye thank?"

"You could tie him up without putting him in there!"

"Mayor, I is Shurff an' I ain't seen m' pay yet. Don't you fret, I'll see he's fed and stretches his laigs. Swede'll proffer his leftovers. This man has stabbed a man, he's got to pay."

"You've thought it all out have you?"

He nodded: "Ah reckon we'll requar that circus jedge," he said solemn with his decision.

I looked at him. "Jenks," I said, "I remember when you used to sleep most of your days and here it is not dawn and it's clear to me you're a changed man, thriving on his duty."

He grinned. "Y'll write thet letter fer me? Fer thet jedge?"

"I'll think about it," I said.

The night was paling. I walked back toward the cabin in my untucked shirt and my bootlaces flapping. In the dirt against Isaac's porch a man was asleep. On Zar's steps another was huddled over his knees coughing fit to wake the dead. I should have been feeling sympathy for that dealer but I was feeling the pain of my own breathing.

Jimmy and Molly were still asleep. In the aftermath of her great battle he had taken my bunk to be near her if she needed, and the dugout had been left to me. But I was too shaken to lie down again, I boiled some coffee and sat at my desk looking at that letter for Archie D. Brogan, thinking Here rises another morning, a little hotter than the last. If someone from the mines doesn't begin hiring soon, Jenks's wagon will be filled to overflowing. Once there was work, once there was money, I told myself, everything would be alright. It was the promise of a year, a settlement growing towards its perfection. That was my notion but the only thing growing was trouble; and it made me shudder to think whatever perfection was, like the perfection I had with Molly, it was maybe past, silently come and gone, a moment long, just an instant in the shadow of one day, and any fool who was still waiting for it, like he dreamed, didn't know what life is.

I counted the savings in my drawer—some two hundred fifty dollars' worth—and I went out and hired four men who said they knew carpentry, and I sent them on a hunt for wood. The terms were three dollars apiece for each day they took to get up an office for me against the south wall of the cabin. After I did that there was a gathering in front of the cabin and I spoke to a number of people, one at a time. One man said he knew the printer's trade and I gave him backing of seventy-five dollars to start up a press in the town.

Another, an old drover, claimed he knew where if he could get a dozen head of fat prime cattle at three dollars a head, he would have them across the flats in a week and would sell them for slaughter for ten dollars. I told him to go ahead. A couple of people I lent money to straight off at a rate of one percent, and by noon I had gotten rid of all my money except what I needed to keep the three of us.

I went outside and stood up on a box in front of the windmill and I made an announcement to the people that gathered. I said until the roadwork began all water was free to anyone not owning property on the street. "The banner means what it says, boys!" I cried like a true politician. "There's a payday coming for all, but until it comes we'll wait together!" Nobody cheered but I didn't think they would.

In all that time Molly stayed in the back room with the door shut, the boy carrying her cups of tea or some food.

I wasn't finished by any means, I planned to write a letter to two or three of the banking companies in the Territory, asking them to consider opening up a branch in the town. I was tempting myself to ride up to the lodes with Brogan's letter to see if I could commit someone to a hiring date. My mind was teeming with plans to keep the temperature down and the money fluent. Toward dusk Zar came barging in the front door. I had expected him.

"Mayor, what a frand is this!"

"What do you mean Zar?"

"I tell you I shall drill a well and then you cut your water prices. Is this the way a frand does?"

"Why you told me you would drill only for your own use," I said, "I shouldn't think it would matter to you."

"This is dirty business, you are making angry a dangerous man!"

At that moment he didn't look so dangerous. He had on his fancy check vest and kneecoat and a hempen cravat and around it all was his barkeep's apron. He raged on, not even knowing he gave himself away, till finally I said: "Now you listen to me, Zar. You're sending for a well driller? Fine, you'll make it back soon enough, just go right ahead. You can hire out a good half dozen men to put up a windmill for you. While you're at it think up a couple of more jobs so you can give out wages. God knows you've made enough money not to have to sweep your own place."

"What's this?"

"These people are lying around here spending their cash and they're not making any. We're grabbing everything they have—"

"Is this bad?"

"It could be. The Company seems to be taking its own sweet time about the road. Until it gets going we're in a bad position. You can't just take out, you have to put back in too, you're a businessman, you know that."

"I do not make whiskey to give away, frand. I do not tell a man to keep his money so he can spend it across the street."

"Alright, you can still hire some of these people, give them a way of paying for your wares."

He looked at me, his anger forgotten: "Blue, I think you are losing your mind. . . . "

"I have lived around this country a long time, Zar. Take a look at the faces along your bar; if you can't read the meanings you don't stand to last very long."

"They say you are giving away money—"

"I've invested some."

"Blue, frand, I'm sorry I have screamed. You are a sick man."

"You'd better give some thought to what I'm saying—"

He stomped over to the door shaking his head. "Alright," I said to him, "I hope you're hiding your gold in a good safe place."

But when he was gone I had to ask myself: Could I be wrong? Was I running scared? If things were really tight neither the Russian nor any of the others would have to be told what to do. The situation was not all that bad. Isaac Maple, for instance, I knew for a fact he credited anyone who said he knew Ezra, his brother. Every poke came into town, it didn't take him one day to find out how to get by Isaac, all he had to say is he'd seen Ezra, and was it at Bannock or Virginia City, it was all the same, he got down on Isaac's books. . . .

Was this not a way of hoping; or was I just being typical of myself, unable to do something in the morning without regretting it at night?

If Jimmy understood what I had done he gave no sign. Nor did I hear from Molly. I slept well at night, there were no sounds to waken me. In the morning Jimmy dragged in that bathtub from the well and pushed it into their room. He went back and forth with a bucket, I suppose Molly had decided to cleanse herself of what filth she could. When he had filled the tub he sat outside her door, his neck flushed red to his ears and that cursed shotgun across his knees.

Outside the front door there was a crowd gathered —for what? What more did I have to do? And then Archie D. Brogan showed up. He must have pushed aside a few of them, there was a lot of grumbling and a few shouts behind him when the door opened.

"Are you that Blue feller? Mcellhenny tells me you've a letter in my name. Brogan."

I stood up. "That's right. It's been here more than a week."

"Say what?"

"It's been here in my desk a long while—"

"Why that son of a bitch sot, I'll fix his hide, he just now told me last night. Well give it here."

It was clear he was a mine boss. His hat was off but just to fan his face, he was a beefy man in his corduroys and he suffered the heat. I got the letter and handed it to him.

"Too bad you had to make a special trip," I said, "you mostly get your mail up at the camp, don't you?"

"What the hell business is it of yours?" he said ripping open the envelope. And then, as he stood there puzzling out the words his florid face went pale. He stuffed the paper in his pocket and stomped out, leaving the door open wide.

Outside they made a path for him and he walked up the street to Zar's Palace. Bert was standing by the door and I motioned him inside.

"Bert, what's troubling you, what are you doing here?"

"Well, Mr. Blue, the girl is getting big as a melon and we don't have a bed yet for the chile to be born in. I want us to have a real furniture bed, you know how I mean, but I'm already two weeks ahead on my pay—"

"Won't Isaac Maple order on your word?"

"No sir, he knows me. Also, he's been paying my honey wages and I can't—"

"Alright, Bert, listen, I'll loan you for that bed whatever it costs—"

He stammered, he looked sorry he had joined the crowd at my door. He was a fine gawky young fellow and I remember thinking, unwillingly, how just a few years older than Jimmy he was.

"Alright, Bert, you pay me when you can, now listen. That man just walked out of here, Archie Brogan?"

"Sure, don't have to tell me that's Mr. Brogan—"

"Go on back to your place and keep your eye on him. He has a letter I'd give my arm to know what it says. Man has a drink he sometimes talks out loud, you know what I mean?"

"Sure, Mr. Blue—"

"I wanted to say something to him about the road, he could put all these people out here to work if he had instructions, go on now."

I showed him out and closed the door. I had been waiting for the mine boss to come down for his letter; and now that he had my heart pulsations ran so fast I could hardly keep myself sitting down. I bit off some plug and chewed and listened to the noise outside one door and the silence inside the other. The boy was gazing at me. I thought Well let me write Jenks's request to the capital, let me compose my letter to the banking companies. But nothing I could do would matter if the mine didn't lay its road. Why had that note been addressed to Brogan care of the town? Why had Angus said nothing to him for over a week?

I stepped outside and walked quickly up the street to the saloon. Some of those people walked along with me. "I've no news, I've nothing to say," I told them as I walked. "I'm going in for a drink, anyone who'd care to stand me one is welcome to come along." That put them off and I went into Zar's and stood by the bar until I caught Bert's eye.

He put a glass in front of me and poured: "Upstairs,

Mr. Blue, he bought a whole bottle and went upstairs with Jessie."

"Well, this is a working day," I said softly, "he must have something grand to celebrate."

"He said not a word. He didn't even act he knew who I was. Just took a bottle and marched up there with Miss Jess."

Mae came over, pushing her hair back on her temples: "I wish that bastard would hurry up and die. How are you Blue?"

"Mae."

"That goddamn dealer. Two days he's been lying up there bleeding all over my bed. I don' understand ol' Adah, she sits up theah you'd thank 'twas her own man dying."

"Well," I said, "she has a feeling for such things."

"Hell, he's jest a-festerin' away. And Lord if it don't serve him right. First day he was here he wanted me to go upstairs just for the love of it. You hear me Blue? 'Why you cheap bastard,' I tell him, 'I'll go with you and you pay me like anyone else!' And you know he wouldn't? How do you like that for a dealer! One on the house Bertie, if'n you please."

"Where's Zar?" I said.

"Who cares!"

I sipped my whiskey and waited there at the bar, watching the stairs and trying not to look concerned. There were men sitting at the tables, talking, playing small-change poker, but the noise wasn't such you couldn't hear things. From one room above I heard the low moans of that dealer; and from another the sound of Archie D. Brogan singing up a song. After a while Jessie came down. Long Jessie went over to Mae and whispered something and they both giggled.

How many verses of that song I must have listened

to, making out no words, but the Irish of the tune again and again. It would stop and I'd think well now we'll hear no more, but he would start up again, having only paused to wet his throat.

Then, finally, a door opened and down the stairs came the mine boss, lurching and holding the rail tight. He slipped and sat down on the bottom step; and he began to laugh. His face was red and his cheeks shot with thin blue veins. I was over there in an instant offering to help him up and that made him stop laughing. He waved my hand away, muttered something and went out the door. I followed and watched as he threw up in the street. When he was done he wiped his face with a red handkerchief and stalked into Isaac's store, walking sober as a judge.

How clear I call up these moments—even the song he sang, a wild dirge, sings in my ears. A man I never knew! He came out of Isaac's place with a bundle and brand-new saddlebags, stuffed full. He threw it on the back of his mule, mounted, and as I stood transfixed, rode down the street and into the flats.

I watched him a long while. Nobody else seemed to notice his leaving, people were all over the street, the lunch crowd was grouping in front of Swede's tent. I went into the store. Isaac was there toting up figures on a pad. The fat Chinagirl was sitting and resting by the door, breathing with difficulty, her hands on her knees.

"Isaac what did that fellow buy?"

"Weren't that the foreman?"

"It was."

"Well he took some vittles, a fryin' pan, a box of cartridges, matches, a blanket, bottle of castor oil, coupla ounces smokin' tobacco. . . . "

Did I have to be told? Did it have to be in a letter?

The next day miners began coming down the trail, walking with their picks on their backs, riding two up on their mules. They filled the street. Angus Mcellhenny told me: "As long as the payroll kept coming, Blue, we kept diggin' that rock. But I knew weeks ago it wasn't ore we were diggin'. 'Twas only the color."

Like the West, like my life: The color dazzles us, but when it's too late we see what a fraud it is, what a poor pinched-out claim.

TWELVE

OF COURSE NOW I PUT IT DOWN I CAN SEE THAT we were finished before we ever got started, our end was in our beginning. I am writing this and maybe it will be recovered and read; and I'll say now how I picture some reader, a gentleman in a stuffed chair with a rug under him and a solid house around him and a whole city of stone streets around the house—a place like New York which Molly talked about one night, with gas lamps on each corner to light the dark, and polished carriages running behind the horses, and lots of fine manners. . . . Do you think, mister, with all that settlement around you that you're freer than me to make your fate? Do you click your tongue at my story? Well I wish I knew yours. Your father's doing is in you, like his father's was in him, and we can never start new, we take on all the burden: the only thing that grows is trouble, the disasters get bigger, that's all.

I know it, it's true, I've always known it. I scorn myself for a fool for all the bookkeeping I've done; as if notations in a ledger can fix life, as if some marks in a book can control things. There is only one record to keep and that's the one I'm writing now, across the red lines, over the old marks. It won't help me nor anyone I know. "This is who's dead," it says. It does nothing but it can add to the memory. The only hope I have now is that it will be read—and isn't that a final curse on me, that I still have hope? I would laugh if I could, who will come here to find my ledgers of scrawls: that old toothless drover who took my savings to bring back beef on the hoof? If he wasn't a liar he was old enough to be smart. I think I knew he was lying when I gave him the money. I was paying him a debt, I was paying him to leave. Maybe the circuit judge ... although now I'm not clear in my head whether I wrote Jenks's letter or not, did I give it to Alf or not, and anyway why should he come by since nothing is left to judge?

Jenks let free that bent-over fellow the minute he saw what chance there was. The hunchback scuttled off in the crowd, I caught a glimpse of him later, he was one of those looting Isaac's store. At least I think so. In all that noise I can't be sure what I saw, there was moonlight hot as the sun, bright as noon, but it was like the light of pain shining from the blackness.

"Jenks!" I remember Molly screamed. She had run outside and was standing, waving at the coach coming down the street. The Sheriff was atop his hearse wagon, the door on the side flapping over and shut. Sitting up there with him was Miss Adah and Jessie.

He thought Molly wanted to get on. "Hurry up, ma'am," he said, leaning over to help her, "them bastards is about to cut loose." And I thought too she was climbing up, even though I had despaired of getting her to go. But what she did, she pulled him down from the box and was all over the poor man, holding around his neck, clutching him, giving him kisses, moaning out her words: "Jenks, get him for me, you've got to get him, you have a hankerin' don't you Jenks, I've seen it, a woman can tell. Get him and I'll go with you anywhere. I'll be your natural wife, anything you please, I swear—"

The boy and I were looking on and the two women from up on the box. All the sound was coming from the saloon.

"For God's sake Jenks," said Jessie turning and looking back. "For God's sake will you come on!"

"But ma'am, if'n hew please!" He was trying to get loose of Molly.

"Jenks, just one shot, why the man's a target, why he's just looking to come up dead!"

"Lady I done throwed my star away."

Adah was weeping: "I left him up there, he's still breathin'. I've no call to leave that dyin' man alone."

"Hush up! You dumb old woman," Jessie said to her. "You think that damn dealer is worth gettin' what Mae is gettin'? You want to go back there with Mae and that other one?—Lord God, Jenks, will you come on!"

At the saloon the crowd was spilling back on the porch and into the street. People were trying to see in like a crowd pushing towards the words of a preacher. You could hear Mae's screams. I knew it wouldn't be long and we'd all be suffering Turner, feeling his sermon. When he had come only God knows. He must have ridden down from the rocks, grinning to see such a boom of people; he must have come from the north, on the heels of the miners, he had left that way after all, the scythe swings back.

WOULDN'T I HAVE SEEN HIM OTHERWISE? ALL afternoon I had stood watching the dust roll back from the flats, once the stage came and went it was like a signal, folks were tying up their things, loading their animals and taking the walk. In front of my cabin it was like how many years before at Westport, Missouri, people standing and saying goodbye to each other but with their eyes gazing the plains in front of them.

That old egg lady left, riding a wagon empty but for squawks; a chicken feather floated out behind her. Jonce Early pulled up stakes without so much as a look back. There were other smart ones, a handcart couple walked by with no expression at all on their faces. But most of those people who'd come looking for work, they were not moving beyond the street.

I had looked on too numb to move watching the street fill to overflow. I didn't want to believe it, I wanted to tell Angus he was lying, I had the wild thought that if I ran up the trail and pushed boulders across it, I could turn them back, those miners. It was a farrago, a sweltering of angers. The noise of talk was like a hoarse wind blowing. A miner came up to me and said quietly, "Stage due anytime you know?"

"Why yes," I said with all politeness, "matter of fact it should be here this afternoon."

He spit out some plug and looking at the ground said, "I'll buy a passage, ye don't mind." He gave me a pouch of dust so I took him inside and wrote a ticket. When he left there was another miner in the door. And before long there was a line of men waiting their turn for tickets. They dropped bills into my hand, silver, chunks of high-graded. Through the doorway, over their heads I could see some towners watching.

I wrote slowly, making more contracts than Alf could comfortably carry, and thinking Now isn't this queer how I got through these motions with my hands of ice, how peculiar to be doing business; like I once saw a man who was shot in the heart, he was as dead

E. L. DOCTOROW

as you can be but he walked around awhile before he lay down.

I knew Zar and Isaac would come after me once the truth struck them, they would make me share their suffering. I gave the last man in line his ticket and they pushed in past him, their faces all dismay. They didn't want to believe what their own eyes told them.

"The road Blue, whan shall they make the road!" the Russian kept saying.

"You know these flats out here, the way nothing is growing? Well when it's an orchard of big, leafy trees with each leaf a five-dollar gold piece—that's when you'll get your road."

"It ain't fair," Isaac said, "it's not right. What do I do now, tell me what I'm s'posed to do now!"

"I don't know Isaac."

"I said it would come to this, I knew it would. I'm ruined! Ye sure sold me, ye surely traded me!"

"Maybe so."

"Why I'd have found Ezra by now, I'd be with my brother today but for you!"

"I haven't heard you complaining the past year Isaac. You've done alright."

"Is that right, is that so? Curse your wretched soul! I've put every penny I made into this street!"

"You must stop this Blue," the Russian shook his fist, "you must do something!"

"Shall I put the gold back in the ground?"

"My hotel! My beautiful hotel! From where shall come the customers—"

"Goddamn you both, why don't you let me be! What is it you want of me! Why am I the one always, people come running to me—get out of here, go on get out, I'm as hung up as you, can't you see that?"

"Frand—"

"Why do you think you're bad off? You don't even know! You've made enough money from this town, you've made enough I'll tell you and if you don't have tidy little bundles cached away you're bigger fools than I take you for."

"Blue, please"—the Russian held out his arms and he had this begging smile on his face, I could see that gold tooth of his—"please, we are losing everything."

I had to sit down. I put my hands on my face and I felt my breath on my icy fingers. Those white-faced, black-derbied Eastern sons of Hell! How long had they known—maybe since the afternoon they waited for Alf, fanning themselves and keeping their mouths shut? Someone said they had made tests when they were up there, they had made markings on their charts—a year past! But they'd had their intentions, else why had the Territory Office sent Hayden Gillis? How long had we been waiting for something that was never to be? Even as the street was filling up the ore wagons were carting worthless rock westerly to the mills. Even as I scanned the flats each morning that letter to Brogan was lying on my desk. There is no fool like a fool in the West, why you can fool him so bad he won't even know his possibilities are dead, his hopes only ghosts.

I said: "Get out while you can. Load your wagons and travel, because sure as you're breathing it won't be long and all these people stuck here like pigs on a pitchfork—they're going to set up a holler."

"What's this!"

"A pair of dumb cowboys, that's all you are. Fretting about your property when it's your hides you should be thinking of—"

"What ye mean?"

"God help you what do you think I mean, you got

eyes don't you? This town is a bust. Every man in it has been sold!"

Now what I wonder is why they didn't leave. I saw by the looks on their faces they knew I was telling them right. They had the chance to get out and I can't account that they stayed, that they ran out of my door and went back, each of his selling counter, putting on a face and coddling the customer right past the time it became too late to leave. Will we not believe our disasters? Or was there nowhere they could go? It was the same with Swede too, there was time to pack and move on before the moon rose but he didn't, not even in those last free moments after the man came.

Molly had opened her door to see the fuss, she stood there barefooted with her hair hanging down, she looked like Wrath. By the time Zar and Isaac had run out there was a dawn in her eyes. Color came into her cheeks and she broke out in a smile and she said to the boy, who was standing by her: "Lord, did you ever hope to see such a sight? Mayor, is that you I hear telling people to get on their horse?"

She began to giggle, she was really joyful, it might have been some farm girl laughing at her suitor. "Jimmy I swear, listen to Mayor Blue here, all these people he's been a-wishin' and a-wantin', well here they are and look at him, he's sick, the shit is scared out of him—"

When Alf came along in the afternoon he had from a distance the sight of a town filled with people and he didn't need to be told what was going on. He reined his team a good way out, near the graves, and turned them around the other way before he and his helper started to toss off the freight. Even so they weren't fast enough, miners were running out there, lugging their gear, there was a rush for the stage. I ran out too to say something to Alf but he was in no mood for talk. He grabbed the money pouch I gave him without even counting and climbed up on the box and flung out his whip and off the coach went, groaning, men were all over it like ants. I watched it going and then one man who hadn't gotten a good hold fell off and he ran after for a bit, ending up standing out there waving his fist as the dust covered him.

Here was all this freight, boxes and barrels, standing in the open like wreckage. In my hands was the order list for Alf, and I looked back at the street and tore the paper into pieces. Swede came out, half running, pulling a handcart behind him, and began to load it up. He grunted and sweat ran down from his yellow hair and he picked up those barrels in a hug, those crates, even scooping up crackers where they had spilled out of a box broken open in its fall.

"Damnit," I said to him, "it's not some lady's rug you have to leave clean!"

He began pulling the cart in, it was Isaac's goods more than his own, he leaned forward on the bar like some ass, some dumb ox. I couldn't help being furious at him, I wanted to hit him.

I walked beside Swede, my eyes on the town. It had no earthly reason for being there, it made no sense to exist. People naturally come together but is that enough? Just as naturally we think of ourselves alone. "Listen to me Swede: Gather up your belongings, take the locks off your spokes and you and your woman get out of here. With those bulls you got you'll need a good start. Do you understand what I'm saying?"

"Aaah, ya—"

"Find yourself some other Swedes. . . ."

I had the same advice for Bert Albany. When I got back to the street I suddenly thought of Bert and I sought him out. He was in the crib where they lived, comforting his wife, but nobody was comforting him. At first he didn't want to leave—"Where to?" he said, he felt a loyalty to Zar, but more he was afraid any trip would put his Chinagirl in labor. I said, "Bert don't argue with an old man. Wrap up what you can carry and come with me. No child has ever been born in this town, and that's the saddest thing I will ever know, but it's true and it always will be."

Roebuck, the smithy, had a wagon. I found him ready to leave and I gave him all the greenbacks in my pocket to take on the couple. But when I put Bert and his wife up behind him I said only: "This man has consented to let you ride." And I walked with the wagon through the milling people, stopping at the edge of the flats and watching it go on. "We was doing alright, Mr. Blue," the boy called back, "what happened to us? Where do we go now?" And I saw that little girl turn back to look, a puffy, tear-stained face taking in with her eyes what her mind didn't understand.

Soon there was a string of travelers spread out on the flats. And then, not ten feet in front of me, Angus Mcellhenny was standing, pulling tight the ropes on his mule's load; and though I had known what to tell Zar and Isaac and Swede and Bert my brain was muddled now, and I couldn't believe what was happening any more than they could. I went over to Angus but no words would leave my mouth, I didn't even know what I wanted from him. His pipe was tight in his teeth, he wouldn't look at me.

"You don't tarry, Angus."

"I'm no fool. Ye'll be traveling yerself hae you any sense."

"Angus," I grabbed his arm, "can there still be gold up there?"

He sighed: "That mountain is picked so hollow, why it's holey as a honeycomb, there's nothin' holdin' it up save air. Listen to me Blue, there's maybe a score of men still up at the site who can't bear to be sold out. They'll rot up there tryin' to take it out on the rock."

"It's a property isn't it? The Company will sell it if they can."

"Aye, there's enough fer salt. They will make a Chinaman of some pour soul who will buy the stock and come out and dig. And when he sees what he's got he'll blow out his brains."

Another miner standing near Angus gave a laugh.

I tried to say something but the words choked in my throat. I looked ahead at the endless reaches, lit red in the late afternoon, and I felt the blood drying up in me.

"Blue," Angus Mcellhenny said softly, and he glanced a moment at me, "dinna spook me wi' yer troubles. Goodbye to ye. I know yer feelings fer yer wee town but I canna bear to think on it."

Well that was the moment I asked myself what I was going to do. Everything was come to nothing. You try to dispose of your life to some purpose even though it appears to have none. My savings were gone; if I could get Molly and the boy on the buckboard how far could they go? Like Angus marching away out there among the others was the shambles of the town blowing off in every direction. All afternoon I watched to see who was leaving, feeling the pain of slow torture. But I have always been one for the protraction of misery and perhaps I counted each man who left as one less twist to the final pain. What I mean to say is I never made up my mind to leave, my will was exhausted. When the dusk came on there was a stillness over the town although the numbers were still thick. Men stood around, hardly anyone was moving. Anger, like heat, lay on the dust of the air. Jimmy came running by me, his eyes bulging, his mouth open as if he were about to scream. I looked where he'd come from, and I walked closer to see what I was seeing. From inside Zar's saloon came the sound of one man's haw haw laugh. Tied up at the railing was a bony used-up nag that I saw was once Hausenfield the German's handsome bay.

LOOKING OVER THE DOORS I COULD SEE ONLY HIS shoulders and his hat. But then he raised his head and there was his dark reflection in Zar's fancy mirror behind the bar. Two Bad Men, the Man multiplied. I remember feeling: He never left the town, it was waiting only for the proper light to see him where he's been all the time.

"Hey, who's the boss here," he called out.

Someone pointed to Zar who was standing at the end of the counter.

"Say, friend, come have a drink, it's good pizen ye made, I'll swar—"

Zar didn't move, and in the silence of that packed saloon the man leaned down the bar and shoved a full glass along. It went the whole distance, people stepping back not to block the way; and at the end of the counter it tipped gently on its side, a-making a pool of whiskey that spread and began to drip to the floor.

With a frown Zar lifted the bottom of his apron and began to dab at the liquid. The Man thought that was funny and laughed, and everyone looking on in that steaming glowing room began to laugh with him. Then

Turner stood up to his full height so I could see now that blaze on the side of his face, the peculiar stare of his eye. He had caught sight of Mae and Mrs. Clement, standing shy behind the Russian.

"Hey honey," he said softly but there was no other sound now. "Hey honey," he said crooking his finger. In that moment I could feel my heart tipping, spilling out its shame, its nausea. I had to run from the Trick, I couldn't tolerate it, what other name is there for the mockery that puts us back in our own steps? Here the earth turns and we turn with it, around it spins and we go mad with it.

Inside Jenks's stable I found the mule and led him quickly to the cabin, but not by the street but behind the houses. I hitched him to the major's rig and then I went around to the front and stepped inside the door.

There was no light and I couldn't see. I heard a rustle from the dugout and when I lit the lamp and held it up I saw them both cowering back inside there. Molly had the boy in front of her, he was gripping the shotgun; and over his shoulder she was pointing that knife at me.

"The mule's hitched," I said, "you want to quick take some things and ride out."

"I'll kill you Mayor," she whispered. She stared at me like I was some animal ready to spring, poised with her legs wide and her hand high holding that stiletto. She looked as if it was I who had summoned him up.

"Don't come any closer—"

"Molly in the name of God listen to what I'm telling you!"

In the shadows her eyes had the light of fire.

"Don't you care!" I shouted. "You want it to happen again? You think I can atone more? Take him away from here, you're mother to him, a bobcat'll curry its young, won't you do that, won't you take him the hell out of here!"

The boy stood between us and now he raised the gun a little. "Look at this," I said, "it should make you proud the way you've hexed this boy. Well I'm finished, I don't want him, he's nothing to me, go on the both of you, get out. The rig's yours, the mule's yours, everything—but quit my sight, you've been only misery to me. I rue the day I saw you Molly, I swear I curse the moment I laid eyes on you. Had I known what you was why I would have stood up to be shot, I would have held out my arms to the Bad Man. Shoot true, brother, or Molly Riordan is waiting who will do it much slower—"

And all the while I raged I could see I had no name in her gaze, this was what she wanted, for the Bad Man to return! She'd been waiting for him, a proper faithful wife. Nothing mattered to her, not me, not Jimmy, just herself and her Man from Bodie. I was ready to kill her.

And the boy standing there like he thought he was her son, it filled me with disgust. "What do you think you're guarding there sonny, something worth the trouble? You think she cares a damn for you? Why she thinks no more of you than she does of me, right now she wouldn't know if you put that muzzle in your eye and squeezed the trigger. Tell him Molly, he don't believe me. Why you're a simp to stand there, you ain't got half the sense of your daddy, you did and you'd be riding away right now!" I said, "Go on Jimmy, get out of here while you can, you don't need her, you're not the first she's fooled, it's no shame. Go on, boy. Go on—"

But he only raised the barrel a little. Well I'm thankful for that, there was not a flicker of belief in his eyes. What he was to do was not my reckoning, it burst from him with the force of shot, he was a long time in the squeeze. How I failed is how Molly did not fail, and in the miserable waste of our three lives I want to declare only for my own guilt.

Now in all this and what followed only once did it strike me to overcome both of them, hustle them on the wagon and take them away myself. It was at this moment, with no thought as how it could be done. I lunged at Molly over the boy's outstretched arms almost at the same instant she heard the coach coming down the street. She crouched and came up past me, swiping at my ribs with the stiletto, putting a rent in my side—and she was out of there while I was stumbling over the boy.

That was as close as I came. Afterwards I hadn't the time.

"JENKS," SCREAMED JESSIE, "IN A SECOND I'M driving this thing myself, Jenks—"

"Now," Molly was cooing, "here you tell me Mr. Jenks will run and just one man he has to take care of?" Her voice was as soft and natural as a sane woman's. "Why Sheriff, I know you can shoot the balls off a man quick as a blink. You're not runnin' Sheriff, no sir, it makes no sense. Look here, even this shit yellow spine of a mayor ain't running."

"That's his business, please ma'am, the way I see hit I can't shoot all those people down in much health."

"Just *him*," Molly gripped his shirt again, "just him, just that Bad Man from Bodie, you know what he did to me, you have any idea?"

"Well—"

"Jenks I promise good things, I swear, I can do more than those two on the box put together. Do you believe that?"

That brought Miss Adah out of her daze. Everything Molly had been saying suddenly made her stand up and point her finger: "Why I always knew," she said with a voice of surprise, "yes I did, even when I passed on my wedding dress to you, that you was no lady."

Down the street someone near the door of Zar's Palace turned and saw the woman's figure atop the coach. He said something and then a few men had separated from the crowd and were running toward us, shouting. The Bad Man was putting a match to everyone.

"Oh Lord, Jenks—" Jessie screamed, and she took up the reins. The Sheriff started to climb to the box but Molly grabbed his arm. At the same time I found myself slapping the horses' rumps just as Jimmy did, although I think we had different reasons. And off lurched the coach, Miss Adah falling back on the roof.

The wheels spun up a cloud of blue dust under the moon. A minute after they were gone, three or four men hooted by on their horses, giving the chase, choking us standing there, flattening us against the cabin wall. I never saw either of those women again and I don't know what happened to them.

"Oh lookit thet!" said Jenks. "Godamighty," his voice broke, "lookit what hew done to me!"

Molly giggled: "Sheriff honey, you'll listen to me now, won't you?"

I'm trying to put down what happened but the closer I've come in time the less clear I am in my mind. I'm losing my blood to this rag, but more, I have the cold feeling everything I've written doesn't tell how it was, no matter how careful I've been to get it all down it still escapes me: like what happened is far below my understanding beyond my sight. In my limits, taking a day for a day, a night for a night, have I showed the sand shifting under our feet, the terrible arrangement of our lives?

I can't remember her foul words, poor Molly, what she said to Jenks, but only that it kept Jimmy rooted where he stood; and that by and by Jenks was spinning his Colt and checking each chamber, his simpleton pride rising like manhood to her promises. Or did he really believe he could stop the riot by killing Turner? At the far end of the street a bunch of men were running out of sight toward John Bear's cabin. Next to the saloon Isaac's store was locked and dark, but already someone was banging on the door.

In those moments I was unable to act. The way I am, I will do as well as anyone until a showdown. But also I was raging that Jenks could believe this woman cared for anything but herself and the Bad Man. The wolfy fool licked the syrup of her words and was marching up the street almost before I could run back inside and get my gun from the drawer. Molly ran in the dugout, already praying with that cross of hers. Jimmy, holding the shotgun slack in one hand, was in a stupor. "Get back inside!" I said to him.

I ran to catch up with Jenks: "You know what you're doing?"

He was trotting like a hero: "Reckon," he allowed himself to say. I wasn't worth too much of his attention now Molly's declarations were in his ears.

"Well I hope you find it worth it, Mr. Sheriff," I said. "But you better have a plan!"

"Stay back—"

"You're a damn fool. He won't give you the time to

sight. This ain't a target to shoot, this is a Man from Bodie!"

"I kin get 'm awraht."

I wanted to believe him. On the left side of the street one side of Swede's tent was buckling and there was the clatter of pots and kettles. I could see now to the end of the street and in the bright blue shadow they were knocking John Bear's shack to pieces. I thought Yes, can one shot do it? It will scatter the flames and the fire will go out.

THIRTEEN

THAT WAS THE IDEA I HELD ON TO LIKE MY LIFE, IT moved me to action, it was a clear simple thought and I took it over from Jenks, becoming the fool he'd been, lifting the fool's hat from his dead body to fit on myself, becoming Molly's final fool, as I am now. But who could not in the face of such ruin, with the race burning crazy in that moon's light? It was justice to kill him, the single face, the one man; I had to do something and what was most futile made the most sense. It was a giving in to them all, every one of those accursed people rolling over each other in the still warm dust of the street, scampering this way and that to find what to destroy.

But I wasn't going after it the way Jenks did. He marched up the steps holding his polished pistol and he pulled one of the saloon doors back. "Hey!" he cried, raising the gun to sight, but the flood of light from inside made him blink, and what easy game he was bathed and blinking against the dark. After a great second's silence there was a rush for the door, men stumbling outside, their shadows looming long on the lighted porch, down the steps, shadows turning into men in the street. Jenks was knocked off his balance, he tried to right himself, his gun hand was swinging wildly.

I heard Zar's voice, "No, no!" and maybe the Russian was going toward the door thinking in a panic of the mirror in back of his bar, or the lamps hanging so grandly above the sawdust. I think it was Jenks's wild shot which caught Zar in the stomach. From inside the Bad Man's gun sounded twice, but Jenks was hit twice, the first shot took him in the chest and spinned him around, the second surely broke his neck. Jenks did a clown's tumble down the steps and there he was twisted double, his face in open-mouthed surprise looking up at me from under his arm.

He's still there, they're all as they are. I can write with one hand but I can't dig. Horses shied away from his fall, a man was running toward me, I thought What is he going to tell me? but he had a barrel stave in his hand. I held up my gun and he veered off like a dog on a richer scent.

Across the street Swede's restaurant was a pile of canvas, humping and shifting, a living thing. He was pulling his wife out from under and I ran over and helped him. We put her on her feet and she grabbed Swede and held on to him, sobbing and hugging him. He was crying too, holding an iron skillet in his hand, his anger making him cry, and when it got the best of him he broke out of her grasp, cursing, and started to beat at the movement under the canvas, swinging that skillet with all his strength.

Helga pulled at him, trying to get him away. People were running every which way, meeting and grappling in the street. It was a lunatic town.

"Swede," I cried, "get her out of here!"

He came to his senses, I have a glimpse now of his face suddenly calm under its shock of hair, white in the moon's color. He picked up his wife and walked away quickly, straight out past the sump, going toward the shadow of the rocks.

From Zar's Palace issued a woman's rising voice of moans stopping short in one deathly scream.

I had remembered a bale of barbed wire standing behind Isaac's store, a big spool of it, maybe Isaac from Vermont had been expecting the herds to come to Hard Times. I made for it, proud of my cunning; and I was in such a fever with my idea, the tear in my side didn't hurt, nor the thought of Molly and the boy awaiting what might be, nor the moment's glimpse I had, going down the alley of the looters beating down Isaac's door. Through the walls of the saloon I could hear Turner begin to sing drunkenly, throw the furniture around—and it was thrilling to concentrate my hate.

Now from that spot there was a clear view to the rock hills lying under the moon as far east as the eye could see. I have the image in my mind of John Bear looking on from a ledge up there, although I'm not sure now this was the moment I spotted him. What can I say, he had no hat or shirt as he waited there on one knee while the mob wrecked his shack, by then he had no reason to wear white men's clothes. I can't understand how my eye found him, he was so still. But the moon picked him out for me, it was a lye moon etching him on my brain. There was motion in his stillness, something already done in his pose, and although I was not to see him again there is no break in the picture I have between then and this morning when I found the Russian on the floor by his bar.

Plotting for the Bad Man I couldn't have understood John Bear last night, if I'd known what he was contemplating it would have made no sense to me. I was dragging that heavy spool up the alley in sweat and in pain and in righteousness. I saw Swede return, striding heavily toward Isaac's store, and I called him and made him help me with the burden. "Ezra!" came Isaac Maple's cry from within his store, "Ezraa-a-a!" out of the cracks and crashes from within and the agonized Swede wanted to go help him, but I kept him with me, infecting him with my madness, and like penitents hurrying before God's wrath we made a bed of barbs on the porch, a trip wire from one post to the other, unwinding the roll, pushing it back and forth, back and forth, as Turner sang.

Swede had a length of planking and with it he climbed atop the overhang and lay flat, waiting; while I stepped back into the street feeling the moon's light like a desert sun on my back. Behind the man's horse I crouched, Hausenfield's bay—a friend, like me, spurred to its bones—and "Turner!" I cried out. "Do you dare come out, Turner!" screaming his name again and again, the voice in my throat someone else's, some stranger's voice doing my work while I watched quietly as one by one the gas lights inside tinkled out and the saloon became dark. Then I shut up. My fingers squeezed out the slack in the trigger, my arm rested across the man's own saddle, with my other hand I held the bay's ear twisted tightly in my fist. In the great silence between that saloon door and me there was no movement. But all around there was riot: people were banging on sheet iron, attacking Isaac's rented boxes down the street; someone was trying to get his wagon going but his horse shied and reared; it was the moment I saw, from the corner of my eye, the hunchback scuttling out of Maple Bros. store with his arm laden, a roll of yard goods streaming out after him.

Well he had the darkness he wanted, if he'd kept the light he might have seen the wire, but he needed to know where I was, where he'd be shooting. He came out, those doors snapping back against the wall, just a shape, a shadow with a hole of fire in its center. Even before the thwack in the horse's side I had let go my shot. I heard a roar of surprise and saw him fall cross the porch, a shadow becoming a man hideously stuck on those infernal barbs.

It is so easy if you have the conviction. I stood up and fired two more times, missing him but not caring, feeling the wonder of the event like a child. A fine spray of blood from the bay's neck covered one side of my face. I could taste it. The Bad Man was trying to get off the wire, but I had hit him in the leg and he couldn't raise himself. Swede didn't have to swing down with that plank, he hung over the edge trying to bash the Bad Man but there was no need, his reach was too short. "No, Swede!" The man turned over on his back on his bed of barbs and shot straight up through the wood.

Swede slumped where he lay, dying like he would, with no sound. This morning Helga came back to the street from her hiding place. She called him and looked everywhere, poking at bodies in the wreckage, but she didn't think to look up. Then she caught sight of those long arms hanging over the edge of the porch top, that head of yellow hair—and for a long while she screamed at him to come down. Swede dead was one of my blunders, one of the last great ones in my life of blunders beginning when I came to this land. I clubbed the Man from Bodie till he was insensible but it didn't help Swede.

And then you see that wasn't my last blunder at all, for I didn't kill Turner I stopped too soon. It was still the Trick that made me cry out my misery and feel the shame of my being. Had I finished my work I would have only damned myself. All around the fights were going on, miners and towners trying to cripple and kill one another, hate riding their voices, gleaming on their knives, imprinted behind their running boots. And none of it had to do with Turner. He was just a man, my God! I felt his weight, I felt the weight of him over my shoulder, I smelled the sweat of him and the whiskey, it was blood that ran from his head and matted his hair. He had lost part of a staring eye on the barbs, his leg was broke, all my senses were glutted with him, I held his wrists together in my hands, and stumbled past that patient horse standing in the street and bleeding to death—and what else but the continuing Mockery could have given me the strength to tote him to the cabin?

"Alright Molly? Is it alright now? Is this what you wanted Molly?"

But she didn't hear me. She stood against the wall as far away as she could and watched me drop him on the table. I could hardly catch my breath, I thought my head would burst and I remember falling and crawling to the cabin door and leaning my back against it because I felt if lay down I would never be able to get up again. And I wish now I could not have seen what happened, or if I had to see it that my mind could split me from the memory. I would like to die on some green somewhere in the coolness of a tree's shadow, when did I last sit with my back against a tree? The wish is so strong in me, like a thirst, I believe I must perish from it. When I think that Ezra Maple might have put him up on his mule and ridden him off to learn the storekeep's trade; or that I might have taken him away myself, in those first hours, before Molly ever put her hooks into him, a carpenter's son, just a hollow-eye orphan—a groan pushes through my lips like my ghost already in its Hell before I am dead. Helga walks up every few minutes, her hair hanging straight down, and she stands gazing at me with her mad eyes while she slowly tears her dress to tatters. Is it Molly again, those eyes? Is it all the eyes of those dead faces? I mean no man has ever had such a watchfulness of dead faces, I have farmed the crop of this country, the land's good yield along with Men from Bodie.

I told him to get by the door for it wouldn't be minutes before the looters would reach us. I said with what breath I could gather, "Jimmy, over here, stand here with that gun." But he was looking at her as he'd been looking for the year or more, he couldn't do anything but look at her. It was his suffering, it was what she demanded.

What caution was Molly's, what disbelief as she slowly moved toward Turner, the man of her dreaming, the great insulter, lying helpless in his own stinking juices on the eating table. Yes it was him alright the same one sure enough by God it was him and no need to wave her cross for protection, a knife would do, the stiletto, *now* she would use it. A jab to see if he was still alive, a gentle stick to hurt him awake, and he flinched and groaned. Back, she jumped and then forward into another place and he tried to writhe away from the point. "Eh?" says Molly. "Eh?" as if to say remember me? remember your Molly? "Eh?" does this make you remember, or this, or this!—almost dancing with the grace of retribution.

"Molly, oh Lord, Molly stop it, stop it—" I shouted stumbling up, going for her. It was an endless frenzy, I cannot describe what she was doing, God have mercy on her, I saw the boy's horror, for how many endless moments did he endure it? And how else could he speak, finally, when he had to call her and claim her as a right? How else could he make the sound of his need, create it true again? He spoke as she had taught him, manfully, with the proper instrument, booming of birth.

It was the moment Turner's arms had closed around Molly as if in embrace. My hand was over the muzzle of the gun but the blast killed them both. Fainting, I could hear people outside tipping over the water tank, and it was that sound I listened to, the spread of water, an indecent gush.

FOURTEEN

Aꜱᴅ ɴᴏᴡ I'ᴠᴇ ᴘᴜᴛ ᴅᴏᴡɴ ᴡʜᴀᴛ ʜᴀᴘᴘᴇɴᴇᴅ, everything that happened from one end to the other. And it scares me more than death scares me that it may show the truth. But how can it if I've written as if I knew as I lived them which minutes were important and which not; and spoken as if I knew the exact words everyone spoke? Does the truth come out in such scrawls, so bound by my limits?

But for Helga I have the town to myself, who's not dead is scattered over the plains. The air is hot, and dry and still. The light of the sun parches me, my mouth is filled with dust, I cannot make spittle. There is no wind to stir the welcome banner, not a cloud. Only the flock of buzzards—sometimes rising, fluttering from some imagined scare—makes an occasional shadow. The street is busy with the work of jackals and vultures, flies, bugs, mice. Together they make a hum of enterprise.

I can forgive anyone but myself. The way I'm facing I can see out over the flats as the afternoon sun bakes colors across them. Who am I looking for, Jimmy? He's gone, he's rising hard, that mule and rig will take him places, another Bad Man from Bodie, who used to be Fee's boy.

I seem to remember a man saying once they would

build a railroad along the wagon trails west. It will bring them along the edge of the flats with their steam engines. I can see if I peer hard enough, I can see those telegraph poles up there like stitching between the earth and sky. Am I dying that slow?

This morning, before I started this, when the pain was too much to sit with, before my arm turned numb, I walked up and down seeing the fruit of the land. Isaac is dead in his store. In the rubble of Zar's Palace that Mrs. Clement is dead although I don't see a mark on her. The dealer must be upstairs. Mae is lying across a table, her dress pulled up around her neck. Her skull is broken and her teeth scattered on the table and on the floor.

In front of his bar lies the Russian, scalped expertly. The bullet he got was in his stomach—a red stain over his apron—he must still have been alive when John Bear reached him. As much as anything it was the sight of Zar, who once struck the Indian from behind, which got me to take my books out here and sit down and try to write what happened. I can forgive everyone but I cannot forgive myself. I told Molly we'd be ready for the Bad Man but we can never be ready. Nothing is ever buried, the earth rolls in its tracks, it never goes anywhere, it never changes, only the hope changes like morning and night, only the expectations rise and set. Why does there have to be promise before destruction? What more could I have done—if I hadn't believed, they'd be alive today. Oh Molly, oh my boy ... The first time I ran, the second time I stood up to him, but I failed both times, no matter what I've done it has failed.

Helga is standing here, she will watch me die. Who will take care of Swede's wife? The mortal stench is everywhere, especially on me, and there is so much carrion in this town I wonder every buzzard on the land won't be here before the sun sets. It has crossed my mind to set the street afire—that would scatter them. But there's no wind and it would be hard work, harder than I can do.

And I have to allow, with great shame, I keep thinking someone will come by sometime who will want to use the wood.

ABOUT THE AUTHOR

E. L. Doctorow's first novel, WELCOME TO HARD TIMES, was published in 1960, followed by BIG AS LIFE (1966); THE BOOK OF DANIEL (1971), a National Book Award nominee; RAGTIME (1975), winner of the National Book Critics Circle Award; LOON LAKE (1980); LIVES OF THE POETS (1984) (called by *The New York Times* one of the best books of the year); and WORLD'S FAIR (1985), winner of the American Book Award. A play, DRINKS BEFORE DINNER, was produced at the New York Shakespeare Festival Theatre in 1978 and has since seen production in regional and university theaters all over the United States. Mr. Doctorow's work is published in over twenty languages. He lives in New York.